THE PRISONER
OF THE RIVIERA

DISCARDED

To Jamie and Shanna

Francis Bacon was a major twentieth-century British painter. He really did live with his old nanny and his ultra-respectable lover, and he traveled to France with them both after the Second World War.

But his adventures in this novel are imaginary, and the various members of the French Resistance and the Milice, the gangsters, cops, and denizens of the Riviera café society are all pure fiction.

THE PRISONER
OF THE RIVIERA

CHAPTER ONE

The war was over; Herr Hitler was dead; Hirohito was mortal. We had flags and bunting, and I got marvelously drunk and committed a public indecency in Hyde Park—my little contribution to Britannia's celebration. Really, the least I could do, and pretty much the most, too, because for all our relief, peace left a lot to be desired. We'd thought that once the blackouts and raids stopped, and the V2 rockets and the casualty reports disappeared, we'd go back to normal life, prewar normal, that is. Turned out postwar normal was what we'd gotten, with dust and disruption, rebuilding and demolition, even slower transport and the rationing of everything under the sun.

It always seemed to be wet, too, and cloudy when it wasn't.

Rain bucketing down, streets awash, everything gray if not black. Coal smoke in the air and the familiar tang of powdered brick and stone, topped up with attar of wood ash. Amazing how long smells linger; light fades, solids rot or erode, but the smell of destruction is a continuing reminder of disasters large and small, even when the empty lots, the pits, and the piled rubble of shattered landmarks—and the bones of those beneath—are out of sight.

Maybe that's why I'd been depressed, though I'd sold a couple of paintings and had money in my pocket. When I opened the door of the Europa, my haven, my drinking club, my favorite place in all London, I felt disgusted. My friends were there and I didn't want to meet them. Fellow painters were at the bar, and I was bored before they opened their mouths.

You might blame the décor, and I admit that the Europa is far from elegance or even cleanliness. But shabby, I like. Seedy bars, louche clientele, artists off their game, and boys on the game— that's my kind of place. Normally.

But that day, I felt bored and irritable. Even when Maribelle leaned over the counter and called, "So where's my painting, then, cunty?" I could hardly manage a smile.

"Oh, she's out of sorts, is she?" At the Europa, as you might have guessed, I'm always in the feminine mode.

"I need Champagne, Maribelle."

"Don't we all! Frenchies are keeping anything worth drinking to themselves at the moment."

I sat down at the bar and pulled a small paper parcel from under my leather coat.

"For me?"

"With infinite gratitude," I said. That was not, by the way, a rhetorical flourish or a figure of speech. Maribelle had literally saved this bacon at least once during the war and lent metaphorical assistance on many bad nights.

"Let's see the masterwork." This from a red-faced, ginger-haired Scot, another painter, another habitué of the Europa. We're both obsessed with Picasso; we like to chew over the problems of painting postcubism and, in his case, of being a successor to the famous Glasgow Boys.

A rustle of paper. "Well," said Maribelle, and she favored me with a specimen of her inventive profanity. She's a linguistic genius with a tongue that can make the language blush.

"Aye," said the painter. "It's an original for sure. But have you no made her nose a little too short?"

Laughter at this, for the nose takes off from the vicinity of one distorted cheekbone and heads for the jawline. But Maribelle smiled; she has a taste for serious painting. By which I mean painting that does more than coat a canvas with pretty colors and surface details. "I always said you'd immortalize me. Do me in my retirement, it will."

"You like it?"

"It's me to the life." She held it up. I confess that I was pleased with it, even seeing it out in the world, which is always a big test of a painting, especially one seen in the insalubrious light and worse air of the Europa. A little rectangle of darkest blue-purple with big fat, fleshy sweeps of white, pink, green, and brown paint laid across it to make a map of her features, the flesh dissolved by energy and taking flight of her bones. "You're on the house, today," she said, and she poured me a glass of bubbly. Woefully adulterated, of course, but the bubbles were reminiscent.

I lifted the glass, toasted Maribelle, took a sip, and said, "I need to go to France. I hear that they have bread without sawdust, unrationed eggs, real cakes, recognizable meat. I'm sick of ration cards and I want to get reacquainted with cuisine."

"What's stopping you?" she asked, for she knew about my recent sale.

"Nan," I said, but even as I spoke I had an irresistible image of the boat train and of Nan sitting beside me with a hamper for lunch. Arnold would have to come, too, because deep in the Blitz he'd promised me Monte Carlo postwar. Now the war was over and we'd done celebrating and were sick of austerity. With his money and what I'd made off the paintings, I could close the studio, pack away the pictures, and make a run for sun, food, and gambling. "You are an ever-present source of inspiration, Maribelle," I said and headed for the door.

A week later it was settled that we were to be off: a traveling party of yours truly, painter and bon vivant; Nan, my old nanny, mostly blind now but game for anything that will please me without "sending us to the poor house," as she puts it; and Arnold, friend and lover, an older businessman and alderman, leaving his family to squire me and Nan around *la belle France*. That's how it is with Arnold. He's ultrarespectable but with a taste for escape and a yen for his shadow side, which is where I come in. He was eager for the trip right away. "A solemn promise," he admitted, referring to Monte Carlo.

"That should perhaps be an unsolemn promise."

"Dear boy, you are right. We cannot be solemn in France." He asked if my passport was up to date and set about acquiring the tickets.

Nan, on the other hand, was initially reluctant. "Full of foreigners," she said, which was, from one point of view, indubitable.

"And the loos will be filthy," she added.

"The loos *will* be filthy, I grant you that. But the food, Nan, the food will be divine."

"You'd think folk who can manage a soufflé could manage to clean WCs."

"And you'd think people with clean WCs would have fine soufflés."

Nan made a face. She taught me to be logical but doesn't always like it when I am.

"If you're set against it, you could maybe stay with Bella," I said. Bella is her great friend, a fellow nanny whom she always describes as "perfect." That may be so, but although they have tea together at least once a week, her last stay with Bella was not a success. To be honest, Nan, who was the absolute ideal for me, is nonetheless very far from being the conventional item. Both she and Bella can ignore that over tea but not in mutual residence.

"Well," she said as if it was a huge concession, which it probably was, "I do want you to have a good time. We'll make the best of it, dear boy."

"Of course, we will." And I gave her a hug.

So you can see we were in the right frame of mind. Travel should be for pleasure. And for that I was ready, believe me, after the Blitz, when I was an ARP warden and Arnold was a fire watcher. You don't want to know all we saw. Then, when the demolition and blast dust grew lethal and the asthma that had kept me out of khaki threatened to kill me forthwith, we had a dreadful exile in darkest East Anglia. Nothing but fens and fields and silence, with miles between the appalling pubs, with dogs and horses set to ambush my lungs at every turning. I hate the country and its echoes of my childhood. Give me pavement, give me traffic, give me pretty boys on the make, give me French cooking. The sooner the better.

But first there was a delay, which, seemingly innocent at the time, was to change the whole complexion of our journey. Arnold's aldermen duties intervened and then he had some business affairs to sort. We were kept waiting in suspense—something I hate. With or without Arnold, I amused myself with roulette and managed to run up a substantial tab at the gambling club. I was thinking that

I'd be working off my markers with some hideous drudgery next, when something quite unexpected happened.

I say unexpected, because we were still in the postwar phase, where we thought that life, which, looked at closely, has always been of the nasty and brutal sort, would now revert to something better. We must have imagined that the monstrosities of total war would have a cleansing effect. As if! You can see why I have a low opinion of human intelligence, my own included. But that was the mood of the time, and if nothing else, I'm an honest chronicler.

So here's the surprise that occurred as Arnold and I were leaving a very select gambling club in the early hours of the morning. Drizzle, of course, streets wet and reflecting the streetlights—how we'd missed them during the war—otherwise not a glimmer beyond the portico of the club. Another gambler left at the same time; I had an impression of height and thick wavy black hair and a sense of his posture, for he was hunched in a dark blue overcoat as if to hide from his losses. I knew the feeling. I love to gamble; I even find a certain exhilaration in losing, but that's at the table, mesmerized by the wheel, deep in the arcane language of *le rouge et le noir*. When you push off back to ordinary life, your losses come to roost on your shoulders, and the world that was so bright and exciting an hour ago turns to dust. I was certain that's the point the man in the blue overcoat had reached.

He turned up his collar against the rain, and just as he stepped from the handsome marble stairs to the sidewalk, I saw a figure, a mere blur, emerge from the adjoining alley. I put my hand on Arnold's arm, a purely automatic warning, then there was a sort of pop, once, twice, and the man in the blue overcoat staggered and lurched before falling backward. Arnold leaped after the assailant, who ran across the road and jumped into a waiting car.

My old ARP training kicked in. The man was bleeding heavily

from a chest wound. I knelt down beside him, ripped his shirt, and used part of it and my handkerchief to stanch the wound. "Get an ambulance!" I shouted. "Get some towels!"

Arnold ran back up the steps into the club, calling for help. A waiter hurried with clean towels and a blanket, and we rigged the best bandage we could and wrapped the injured man up to stave off shock. His eyes were half closed and his face seemed drained of blood. He was certainly losing a lot. My hands and shirtfront were covered as well as my trousers, and still a wide red pool was spreading on the cement: shades of the Blitz and of blackout calamities. I am well acquainted with calamity, which, pictorially, is one of my favorite subjects.

"Hang on," I said. "Help is coming. Hang on." That's what we ARP wardens always told victims, as if life were a trapeze act that required a death grip on the bar.

His eyes opened then, cold black orbs. His glance was malevolent—but perhaps he was just in pain. He seemed unable to speak, and I warned him not to try, though when the manager, fat, pale, awesomely self-important, came out, he bent over the wounded man—no kneeling in the mess for him—and demanded to know what he'd seen and who'd shot him and was there a car and so on until I told him to shut up. He didn't like that, but there wasn't much he could do because now came a Klaxon and ambulance men arrived in the usual whirlwind of questions and commands with a stretcher, bandages, and vital fluids.

I was so bloody from my exertions that there was a moment of confusion when one of the ambulance men took my arm and asked me where I was hit. "I'm fine, I'm fine," I said. "Look after him. He's hemorrhaging badly."

They gave me a blanket just the same, and Arnold got me back into the club WC where I dirtied half a dozen towels before I got all the blood washed off, my leather jacket wiped, myself dried. I put on the jacket again minus my ruined shirt, and Arnold draped a blanket over my shoulders as if I were a survivor of some liquid disaster. Which, in a sense, I was going to be.

Naturally, there were questions and more delays in our holiday. A respectable citizen shot in front of a semirespectable club was an offense to good order and a little indication of how much the war years had changed London. The police took this personally, and they wanted to know what we'd seen—very little in truth—and alternately implored and impugned our memories. The nice coordination of the shots and the car implied a professional job, but the escape of two witnesses raised certain questions in their mind: *Had we known the victim? Spoken to him in the club? How had we come to leave at precisely the same time?* And so on. We weren't able to give them much satisfaction, though they gave us a great deal of irritation, so much so that, when something curious happened, I did not toddle off to the nearest phone box and call in a report.

That was two days before we were to leave. Boat train tickets resided in Arnold's pocket; Nan had her valise packed; my clothes and a painting kit were in two big suitcases. I was in my studio, a splendid space with a crystal chandelier and wonderful light that had once belonged to Millais, yes, Sir John of hyperrealism and drowning *Ophelia*. Not to my taste, but he knew a thing or two about painting, and he'd left me a good atmosphere, conducive to work. No matter what I do the night before, I am up by six and into the studio by seven a.m. That particular day I was working on a study of a side of meat that I'd seen in the butcher shop. I like painting meat, the yellow-white fat, the wonderful shades of red from pink to purple, the textures of flesh, flayed and otherwise. That's what I do well, though I was having the usual struggle with grounding the shape when I heard Nan at the door.

"He's painting at the moment," she said. "Whom shall I say is calling?"

Oh, ho, I thought, because she had her nanny voice on, very high, refined, and carrying. It's warned me of bill collectors and coppers and time-wasting associates, and I was set to slide through to my bedroom and out the window, when I heard his name. It was Monsieur Joubert, the proprietor of the gambling club.

"It's all right, Nan," I called. Sooner or later I would have to pay my club debts, and maybe I could interest him in a painting, perhaps a portrait. Dodgy characters often have a taste for art.

"Well, Francis," he said, "so here's how you spend your off-hours." And laughed at his own joke. Detestable habit. He wandered around the studio, looking at my work quite uninvited, and stared at a row of small portraits and self-portraits propped up on a shelf. "Unusual, Francis. Unusual." He turned his little porcine eyes on me and nodded.

I disliked the man. At the same time, I could see his swept-back hair, his stubby nose, and flaccid cheeks on canvas. The club owner was a mysterious gent with a provenance like a forged picture. There was an ambiguous accent lurking in his background. He claimed to be French, but I suspected he was Italian or Swiss. He'd showed up near the end of the war, opened the club with considerable fanfare, and attracted an eclectic clientele of toffs, thugs, and bohemians.

"What can I do for you?" I needed to get on with the painting, because I saw now that, while my dark background was not going to work, a certain steely gray-pink was a distinct possibility.

"It's what I can do for you," he said, dredging an oily charm from some nether region. "We are all so grateful for your efforts for poor Victor the other night."

"How is he doing?"

"He's dead." He crossed himself. "But not your fault. No, no, your efforts aroused nothing but admiration. It wasn't blood loss; he took pneumonia."

"It's a murder case, then." I wondered that nothing had been in the papers. But perhaps there had been. I would have to ask Nan, who remembers every scrap of crime news.

"Of course. Tragic," he said, and I feared for a moment that he would wipe a tear, but some remnant of taste restrained him. "Victor leaves a widow," he said and sighed.

"Orphans, too?"

He gave me a sour look. "No, thank the Lord, just the widow. Poor woman." He shook his head and took another turn about the studio. "She will be grateful as well," he added after an examination of one of my screaming heads. "Very grateful, which has made me think of a way to thank you."

I waited.

"You have run up a considerable tab at the club," he said after a minute. "Well, young men naturally like to gamble. But, sad to say, you do not appear to have a large source of income. These surprising paintings—yes, truly surprising—are perhaps not reliable collateral. How sad, the life of the artist, no?"

There was something in that.

"Yet your kindness to Victor! Under fire, at the risk of your own life, surely this is worth something."

"One might think so." If he had an offer, I wanted to hear it.

"Victor left a letter for his wife. Yes, yes, thanks to you, he was able to dictate a last note. She will be so grateful to have such a remembrance, don't you think?"

I nodded, though not knowing the details of their marriage, who could be sure?

"And I was able to assist him in assembling certain papers of a sentimental value for her."

"Very nice," I said.

"Yes. But"—and here he paused and pivoted on one polished shoe; he wore, I noticed, a sort of lounge slipper as black and shiny as coal—"there is some problem with the manner of delivery. I do not like to mail these things to her. I think we need the—what is the phrase—the personal touch."

"Always a good idea," I said, but I guessed we weren't talking strictly sentimental value here.

"I understand that you and your friend are taking a little holiday in France. Might I ask if you are going south?"

I nodded.

"Let me guess!" A quite unnecessarily dramatic pause. Then, as if producing a rabbit from a hat, he said, "Monte Carlo? Alas, our poor club cannot compete with the attractions of Monte! Such a palace, such a clientele! The dream of every gaming impresario! I envy you, Francis. I truly do."

I waited to see what would come from such an elaborate preamble.

"It happens," he said at last, "that poor Victor's widow lives on the Riviera. Perhaps you would undertake to deliver his papers to her?"

I shrugged. You could make fish soup just off the smell of this.

"I think as a little thank-you for your help to Victor—and to his widow, of course—we could forget your debts at the club." He pulled out some slips and showed them to me. All together they totaled an awesome number of pounds and guineas. "When I hear from her, I tear them up, yes?"

I didn't have much choice unless I wanted to be working for the club for the next decade, but before I could answer Nan piped up from the kitchen. "Have him put it in writing, dear boy."

Joubert frowned, but he scribbled a note and signed it. Nan sidled in, slid the paper into her black leather nanny's purse, and retired to the kitchen, whereupon Joubert produced a substantial packet from one of his coat pockets. Victor's letter must be nearly the length of a small book. The wrapper was very carefully taped up and sealed with a couple fat daubs of red wax. "I needn't tell a gentleman of your intelligence that the seals must remain unbroken."

"Do not offend me, Monsieur." I tried for righteous indignation, but I was already wondering if I could take just the smallest peek at the contents.

He bowed with a particularly oleaginous and unconvincing smile, and Nan reappeared to usher him out.

"A dubious man," she said when the door was closed and locked. "And no gentleman."

"I should think not."

"What do you suppose is in it?" She picked up the packet.

"Why, Victor's last letter to his wife," I said. "Supposedly."

"Victor. What's Victor's last name?"

"Renard. Supposedly."

"Who was shot outside that club?"

"The same. It was in the papers."

"But not his death, dear boy. I would certainly have noticed his death. Either you or Arnold has read me the *Telegraph* every day since. I shouldn't like to think that the *Telegraph* has let us down."

"Nor I, Nan."

"But there's money involved," she said, peering at Monsieur Joubert's note. "We must have a look in that package."

"Sealed up like King Tut's tomb."

She poked at the wrapper with her long bony fingers. "A book, I think, with a soft binding like a notebook."

I took the package from her. I could feel the outline of what, yes, felt like a notebook. With maybe some papers. Maybe a letter, after all, maybe not. "Have we got any sealing wax?"

"I think so, dear boy. But the seal?"

"We'll make a copy," I said, "with a little plaster mold."

That's what we did, but several hours of careful work proved disappointing. The letter was just as Joubert had said, a short farewell note in shaky handwriting expressing love and regret and including a reference to good times in the past. The text struck me as curiously flat and pro forma for someone's dying words, but no doubt the writer hadn't been too concerned with style. Odd just the same, and the notebook, likewise, with its columns of figures and names, mostly but not exclusively French, along with some notations in no language I recognized.

When we had rewrapped the package in brown paper and sealed it up with cellophane and red wax, Nan said, "Get rid of it as soon as you can."

How sad that excellent advice is so readily ignored. As soon as we were on the Channel ferry, I felt free of my usual concerns—always a delightful, if dangerous, sentiment. And then France was so different. Though Caen was said to be utterly destroyed and we saw damaged fields and shattered churches, Dieppe looked like a prewar town. From the boat train customs shed, I saw cranes aloft over the port and wagons and trucks loaded with timbers to repair the docks, but the town itself seemed almost untouched.

"Is there much damage?" Nan asked. That was to be her question throughout.

"The port, yes, the town, no. Everything seems intact."

"The Canadians died here," Nan said. I used to think that her mental map of two conflicts was part of her eccentricity. Now I know better. There are parts of London forever marked for me, places where I smell blood, smoke, and gas.

When I said, "We must eat and drink for them," she patted my arm. And, though she is dead suspicious of foreigners and distrusts the French and asked if every plate was clean, she tucked into the bread and a nice piece of plaice, while Arnold and I gorged on mussels with garlic and butter. We'd come to enjoy ourselves, and we did, both there and in Paris, where we wondered at the clean streets and clean air, at the intact buildings and the handsome blocks lacking the craters and gaps so much a part of London. As we wandered down the Champs-Elysées, I described the sights to Nan: the Arc de Triomphe, the lines of chestnut trees, the palaces and museums, and the French taxicabs, which Nan associates with the World War I Battle of the Marne.

"No damage?" she asked again, for she distrusts the French whom she feels did not quite do their part.

"Splendor saved by capitulation," Arnold murmured.

I had to agree, though whether it is really better to keep your buildings and have Nazis in your bed than to lose your buildings and keep *der Führer*'s boots across the water, I don't know. But I was sure there would be plenty of damage under the surface, flesh and blood and moral equanimity being less durable than stately monuments. Certainly there were plenty of boys around Pigalle with thin, hungry faces. Thanks to my uncle Lastings, who deprived me of my innocence then abandoned me to profit from my knowledge, I'd been in their shoes between the wars, and I didn't mind sharing the wealth. Paris presented opportunities such as I am quite willing to take, but, after Nan and I nearly made ourselves sick on filled pastries and fancy cakes, we took the Train Bleu south to the sun. We had in mind extravagant fun—and, of course, the delivery of Victor's "last words."

CHAPTER TWO

We'd planned for a leisurely course along the Riviera, an orgy of French food and seaside casinos on our way to Monte. What I hadn't taken into account was Nan's failing sight, which made navigating unfamiliar places difficult. My heart sank when I heard her stumbling into furniture in her adjoining room or watched her listening at the curb for traffic or extending her hand for fear of street trees and lampposts. She admitted to being half blind, but she managed so well at home and around the studio that I hadn't realized how much she relied on memory. Although she never complained except about the multitude of foreigners and the filthy public lavatories, Arnold agreed that moving her every day or so was going to cause her difficulty. We decided on our mandatory stop for Victor Renard's widow, if such she was, then straight to Monte Carlo.

Fortunately, the Widow Renard lived outside what turned out to be a particularly attractive resort. A row of white and pink hotels equipped with gay awnings and classical façades overlooked a sandy shore and a palm-lined esplanade that ended at the casino. Arnold was taken with the beach, and I had to admit that the tourist area with its landmarks would be easy for Nan. We took a decent win at roulette as an omen and booked for a week at the best hotel in town.

Ah, to be *en vacances* as the French say. Have I mentioned that I hate the shore? At least the English shore. The cold and fog, the tacky amusement piers and argus-eyed landladies are not my style. But sun and French bread and good pâtés make up for so much, and soon I devised a routine that pleased me. I usually stayed in to paint until late morning, when I would make my way across to the *plage*. Arnold would be sitting after his swim, smoking and reading something serious, which he would share with me, because he wants to complete my education. Arnold is big and robust with a broad forehead; a straight, rather thin nose; and a round chin. He is not handsome exactly, though his hazel eyes are good, but he is vigorous and considerate and, at nearly twenty years my senior, just the right age for me.

Yes, though pretty boys are fun, I prefer older men. We get on very well, and he is genuinely fond of Nan, who I always find sitting beside him, wrapped up like an Edwardian lady under an umbrella the size of a marquee. Nan can't read anymore—either Arnold or I must read her the British newspapers that we buy at the kiosk—so she watches the waves and the boats and critiques bathing costumes that are all too skimpy in her opinion. I lie on a straw mat and look into the blue nothingness and soak up the sun we all crave or splash in the water with Arnold, who is an excellent swimmer. That's morning, which ends with a long lunch at the restaurant overlooking the esplanade and the shore.

Afternoons are already warm—hot for us northerners. We take siestas like the locals, and Arnold and I amuse ourselves in bed. Then, around about four, when the shops start to reopen, I take myself off to the upper town for a drink in one of the cafés or for a walk into the dry hills with Arnold. The buff and gray landscape is bracing, and there's little pollen to bother my asthma. The sea below is a bold blue-green and the bleached hills and the vivid sky and water remind me of my Australian pal, Roy, whose Antipodean palette echoes just those hues. I wonder if mine reflects London as clearly.

At night we eat well again and hit the bars and the casino after Nan goes to bed—or, as she's been doing more and more, wins money from the bridge players in the lobby, who foolishly think a half-blind ex-nanny will be an easy mark. About the only thing I don't do is visit the Widow Renard. The packet lay under the clean shirts in my suitcase, ignored rather than forgotten. I had a strong sense that the package was bad luck and my errand, bad business. If I'd had cash in hand, I'd have chucked it into the sea. As it was, I left delivery until the day before we planned to leave, and then I postponed it again until late afternoon, when I walked up to the station and took the train down the line to the fishing port near Madame Renard's rented villa.

The local rattled along the Mediterranean, brilliant ultramarine in the late-afternoon light. I got out at the village: a cluster of houses with a little hotel next to the station and a café between it and the fishing port. Madame Renard's house, the Villa Mimosa, was up in the hills, and I was directed to a steep road that shortly lost its tarmac and became stony as well as vertiginous. The land was dry and rocky with insects buzzing in the dusty scrub. As I walked, long gray shadows reached down from the hills to darken the desolate landscape that made such a contrast to the pretty coastal towns.

After I'd climbed a mile or so, I reached a hamlet of white and buff houses squatting under heavy tile roofs, one- and two-story constructions with their stucco coatings eaten away by age and weather to show the stone and brick underneath. Everywhere the shutters were down against the heat, and except for a cat asleep in one window and three black hens pecking through the white dust, nothing stirred.

Victor's supposed widow lived in the largest of these buildings, a two-story house no better maintained than the rest but with the pretension of French doors and a walled front garden. I opened the ironwork gate, crossed a bare yard ornamented by two spiky plants and a few dried-up pots, and rang the bell. No answer. I waited long enough to feel relief, and I was looking for somewhere to leave the package, when the door opened with a dry creak. A young woman, barely more than a girl, appeared in the doorway. I recognized her right away—not her personally, but her type, alert and underfed with a bad haircut atop a pert, intelligent face. She wore a black-and-white-striped sailor shirt and tight black Capri pants that showed off nice legs. Her lipstick was bright red, her mascara, purple, and if she was grieving, I was the pope in Rome. But I recognized her. Those of us who have lived by our wits and survived on our looks are all members of one club.

"Madame Renard?"

"*Mais oui,*" she said and looked me over carefully. I was tempted to wink, but Joubert wasn't paying me for comedy.

"Monsieur Joubert sent me. I have a package for you."

She stepped back and motioned me inside the dim foyer. I saw that the room beyond, striped with the thin bands of sun seeping through the shutters, was empty. In fact, as my eyes adjusted from the brilliant white glare outside, I noticed that there was not a single table, chair, or chest visible anywhere and that the walls had been stripped bare. Besides ourselves, the only sign of human habitation was a pervasive smell of Gauloises Bleu. "You took your damn time," she said in French. Her voice was harsh, but her speech, though profane, was not uneducated. A surprise, that.

I shrugged but I wondered how she knew I'd been in the area. Perhaps she didn't. Perhaps living in a house without furniture had gotten on her nerves. Perhaps black wasn't her color. Perhaps she wasn't Madame Renard; she certainly seemed a curious match for Victor, the elegantly dressed gambler, but there's no accounting for taste in erotic matters.

"Let's have it." When I handed over the packet, she stepped into the adjoining room and cranked open a shutter. "You examined this?"

"Certainly not." Fortunately I can lie with a straight face and, in any case, I had learned almost nothing from my examination.

"Wait here." She disappeared into the back, her espadrilles slapping along the tiled floor. When she didn't immediately return, I took a turn along the hall and tried the door behind me without success. A second door opened to reveal another empty, shuttered chamber. I found it hard to believe that anyone was in residence, yet there was a sense of presence. Though I could detect no sound, not even Madame moving about in the back and certainly no voices, I had a feeling that we were not alone, that there were others in the house, that she had gone to take them the packet.

"Ah, Monsieur." She appeared behind me in the corridor, looking relieved, I thought. "It is all very satisfactory. So thoughtful of Victor. I am grateful to you."

She seemed sincere, and I made a little bow.

"He was such a thoughtful man." She sniffed but could not manage a tear. "You were with him near the end, I understand."

"I did my best, but he'd lost too much blood."

"A tragedy." Her face darkened in a reasonable facsimile of grief. "Could I offer you some refreshment? A drink, perhaps?"

Music to my ears, normally, but something about her quick eyes and her theatrical talents warned me not to linger. "Alas, Madame, I am due back shortly. It took longer to reach your villa than I'd expected."

She made a little face. "It's at the end of the world," she said. "But, of course, Victor loved it and so I love it, too. We could drink a toast to Victor."

"Another time that would be a pleasure."

"If we meet again, Monsieur," she said and opened the door.

For a curious moment, I had the feeling that she would like to delay my departure, before she gave a little wave and closed the door smartly.

Outside the gate, the dusty road dropped down to the sea and the little port below, while the hills reared up dark behind me. My first impulse was to hustle back to the station before shadows overtook the track. Then, completely on impulse, I ducked down an alley—one could hardly call it a street—that squeezed between a short row of houses and took me out of sight of Madame's villa. Could there be another road, an alternate track down to the coast and the rail line? I saw a small church with a squat stone tower, found the door unlocked, and stepped inside.

The nave was spartan, a few dozen wooden chairs, a small altar, a choir stall, a large wooden crucifix, and a pervasive smell of old dust and incense. There was a door toward the back, doubtless to the vestry, and, to my left, a second door to the tower stairs. Mercifully, the climb was a short one, because the well-aged dust contracted my lungs. I pushed open the trap and clambered into an open belfry where I had an excellent view of the Villa Mimosa. I stood back from the opening and waited. Five minutes passed, ten. I was wheezing and beginning to feel foolish when the gate opened and two men walked out.

They were dressed like French workmen in overalls and blue smocks, but my guess was that they hadn't done an honest day's work in a long time. For one thing, they were slipping and stumbling just as I had done on the dusty track, and, for another I caught a glimpse of town shoes, not workman's boots. I moved to the other side of the tower and watched them descend. I had half convinced myself that they were on some innocent errand until they paused at the side street. They were looking for me, I realized, and, trapped in the only obvious refuge, I had a bad moment before they continued down the main road and out of sight.

After half an hour, I figured that they must have reached the station, and whether they waited or returned, I wanted to be gone before dark. I clattered down the stairs and out of the church. A block farther on, the houses ended and the street turned into a goat trail through the scrub. Disinclined to meet the faux workmen on the main road, I went with the goats, skittering over loose rocks amid the white powdery soil. I took an hour negotiating various rocky outcrops and thorny bushes to reach the coastal road.

The station and the hotel were visible in the distance, but I was too far away to tell if anyone was waiting on the open platform or sitting at the café. I decided to approach along the shore, well below the road and the platform, and I was about to cross, when I had to wait for an oncoming motorbike towing a loaded sidecar. As it rounded the sweeping curve toward me, the bike hit a pothole. The whole contraption bounced, flinging its cargo onto the tarmac. I caught a rolling bicycle wheel and picked up a second when it came to rest in the gutter.

"Ah, monsieur, merci, merci." The motorcyclist pushed up his goggles and came forward to shake my hand. He had a lean, tanned face below curly brown hair, and he was wearing an unusual costume, a brilliant blue-and-white-striped jersey with very tight black shorts that showed off his strong rump and beautiful muscular legs. His name was Pierre, and he was the just sort of lad I find it a pleasure to help.

He examined the wheels I'd collected, checking the rims carefully, exclaiming profanely all the time about the state of the roads and the inadequacies of his transport. Besides the spare wheels, I noticed some inner tubes and several small cardboard boxes. When he was satisfied that there had been no serious damage, he began to repack, complaining that this was not the first difficulty he'd had on his way from Nice and that these expensive parts needed to be delivered in good shape. "Perhaps some rope," he said and looked around as if a good length of hemp might appear by magic.

I examined the sidecar and had a better idea. "Give me a ride back into town and I'll hold the wheels."

"Monsieur, you are within sight of the *gare*. You could ride in comfort."

I explained that I had a particular desire to avoid the station, that I had suffered a *petit contretemps* too embarrassing to relate, that the *gare* and the estimable SNCF were out of the question at the moment. After some discussion and a Gallic shrug from Pierre, I was wedged into the sidecar with the spare parts and the inner tubes. Pierre handed me the three extra wheels and hopped on the cycle.

Off with a lurch and a fart of exhaust down the straight toward the *gare*. Half screened by bicycle wheels, I whipped by the empty station platform and my two "workmen" in the nearby café. The coast road was narrow and winding, rock on the land side, sand or a drop to more rocks on the other. Despite his earlier troubles, Pierre favored the accelerator and the sidecar found every little imperfection in the road. Any bump brought various boxes and bike parts into connection with my anatomy, while centrifugal force threatened to send me into the rocks or launch both of us into the blue Mediterranean. Without goggles, I mostly had to keep my eyes shut against the wind and flying grit, a circumstance that added to my discomfort.

Now, I quite like excitement, and even danger isn't off the menu, but blind speed and invisible disaster are not to my taste at all. I got brief, frightful glimpses of potential calamity in palms and pink and buff stucco walls and dangerous curbs and a stray dog and two careless pedestrians. It seemed a long while before the motorcycle dropped from a whine to a roar to a throbbing rumble. I opened my eyes as we bounced off a side street into the courtyard of a small bicycle repair shop. Pierre switched off the motor and flipped up his goggles. He had, I now noticed, eyes between brown and green with little gold flecks like a cat's. "All right, monsieur?"

I handed out the wheels and attempted to disengage myself from the tires, the boxes, and what turned out to be a couple of extra bike pedals, one of which had gouged my right shin. I started cleaning up with my handkerchief, but Pierre unlocked the shop and motioned me inside. He took down a first aid kit with iodine, Nan's mainstay, several gauze pads, and reels of tape. While he patched me up, I looked at the photographs on the walls: men in Pierre's blue-and-white-striped kit posed with racing bicycles and, sometimes, with trophies.

This was the local club, he told me, and he was a member as well as the team's official mechanic. The parts were for his team leader's bike, which was getting set up for a big race, and he'd taken the motorbike to save the train fare, a decision that would have been a disaster without me. He was so distressed about my leg that he insisted on riding me down to the front in the sidecar and he was

25

so amusing and decorative that I had him stay for dinner, where he explained bicycle racing and mentioned that the ongoing Tour de France would run through Monaco.

"We will watch for you," said Arnold.

"Oh, Monsieur, I will not be in that race, not even as a *domestique*, but I hope to work as a mechanic on the Riviera stage." Then, sensing our all-encompassing ignorance of this splendid event, he began explaining the extraordinary length and difficulty of the race, the climbs in the Alps and the Pyrenees, and the hundreds of kilometers of stages that comprised a circuit of the entire country. "And the last stage beginning in Caen, Monsieurs, the martyred city—it will be very moving."

In this way, we passed a pleasant evening. After Pierre, who kept training hours, said good night, we remained drinking on the terrace instead of going to the casino or one of our usual bars.

We left early the next morning for Monte Carlo, and it was two days later, after we were established in a pleasant waterside hotel and losing money hand over fist at the casino, that I visited a news kiosk for the London papers Nan enjoys. Almost as an afterthought, I picked up *Nice-Matin*, thinking to check on the progress of the famous bicycle Tour.

Standing under the plane trees in the dappled sunshine, I opened the paper to an article headlined, "Murder in the Var." Just Nan's cup of tea, I thought, with the added promise of the guillotine, for my dear nan has a great passion for capital punishment. I was skimming the story when my chest contracted: the victim was known locally as "Madame Renard." Victor's supposed widow, the woman I'd visited, was dead, and I had perhaps precipitated this by delivering Victor's legacy. It took me a moment to digest that idea, before my shock turned to surprise and then doubt when I checked the accompanying photo.

26

Instead of the Madame Renard I'd met, who was young with short, honey-colored hair and a wide face with broad cheekbones and an impudent expression, this Madame Renard was older, Arnold's age if she was a day. With her long nose and bony cheeks, dark hair streaked white, and the large eyes of a tragic heroine, this Madame Renard looked plausible for the widow of a gambler with enemies, but she wasn't the one who'd collected Joubert's package.

I sat down on one of the benches to read the story carefully. The body of Claudine Renard had been found the previous afternoon when one of her neighbors delivered some eggs, found the kitchen door unlocked, and ventured inside. Madame Renard lay in a small stone pantry off the kitchen with her neck broken. There was no sign of a struggle, and it was as yet unclear if the victim had been killed where she was found. There was no information on the time of death, but I profoundly hoped that it was well outside of five p.m. on the afternoon I rang the bell at the Villa Mimosa, even though earlier might implicate *my* Madame Renard while later suggested that she had met a similar fate. All this was bad in any case.

Worse was to come. The neighbors, who clearly had been alert behind their shutters, reported that the villa had had a number of visitors, some in cars, and at all hours. Although those late-night visitors should have been the concern, the police seemed more anxious to trace the whereabouts of a fair-haired foreigner who had asked directions to the villa on what the paper referred to as "the fateful day." I'll just bet they were. With that thought, I realized what I'd considered a diversion for Nan presented serious trouble for me.

CHAPTER THREE

"Make a run for it," was Nan's advice, while Arnold, reverting to his solid-citizen mode, advised a quick cross-border visit to the nearest French police station. "You saw two men leave the villa. They may be the very ones involved."

Nan shook her head. Her fascination with newspaper crime accounts has given her considerable expertise. "That's risky without knowing the time of death," she said. "And you are guilty until proven innocent here."

"There's no question of that!" Arnold exclaimed, but I thought it very likely that a mysterious fair-haired foreigner, aka me, would look like a nice solution to a sensational murder. And so timely, too, right at the start of the tourist season.

"Then," said Arnold, the voice of conscience and reason, "there's your Madame Renard."

Nan sniffed. "Likely no better than she should be, that one."

"She may also be in danger. You said she looked young and"—he hesitated a second—"down on her luck."

"Off the street in Marseille, I'd venture."

"Expendable," Arnold said.

"So is our dear boy to the *flics*." That's my nan. Her love of capital punishment is balanced by her dislike of authority. What she might have become had she been born male or wealthy staggers my imagination.

"The difficulty is the French border," I said. "The police will have my name soon. If Pierre reads the paper—that's it right there. Or the hotel personnel, even. I did ask about the Villa Mimosa, about the location of the hamlet and the proper train stop."

"Raising another question," said Nan. "Why weren't you given more explicit directions if that package was so important? That Joubert is a jackass."

I was sure that was true, and I feared that one or both of the Madame Renards had trusted him unwisely.

"You were set up," said Nan. "Once you asked for directions."

With this sobering thought, we sat pondering our alternatives. To go to the police, to respond to that call for assistance would be a point in my favor. On the other hand, my description of the two "workmen" and of my "Madame Renard" might well lack corroboration, though the men had been at the café near the station and the neighbors must have seen them as well. It was possible my statement would be taken, my public spirit commended, my vacation resumed.

Possible, yes, but even stronger was the chance of being detained indefinitely in *la belle France*, possibly in a French prison. I wasn't going to risk that. Dieppe and the boat train were out of the question, but I could hop on the local and make for Italy. Arnold and Nan would return via the boat train, and I would get myself north to Holland or Belgium and cross the Channel there.

Arnold thought this plan possible; Nan was enthusiastic. I went upstairs to pack, and I had my paintings stowed and my suitcase ready when there was a knock on the door. Funny how bad events send out their own vibrations. I knew before I spoke that it was not the chambermaid. I looked out at the balcony, but we were on the third floor, and even a successful run would be a confession of guilt. I closed my suitcases and called, "Entrez."

Two men stepped into the room. One was a local policeman in the principality's handsome uniform. He was short and broad shouldered with a physique like a boxer and an athlete's restless grace. He was markedly younger than his companion and dark, with thick, black hair and Italianate features. In better circumstances, I'd have given him the eye. The other visitor was a tall, shambling French police detective with a large, broken nose, full mouth, and small gray eyes, who walked as if his knees and his feet were not in direct communication. Both men were very formal and polite, showed me their identification, and asked for mine. I handed over my passport.

"You appear to be leaving," remarked the Frenchman, whose name was Inspector Chardin. Shades of the great genre painter. Would that prove a happy omen? Probably not, for he seemed gratified to have found me packing like a proper felon on the run.

"Monte Carlo is wonderful," I said with a nod toward the Monégasque, but I have not been lucky at the tables. Besides, I want to visit the police in Menton."

This clearly surprised him. "How so?"

"Why the story in *Nice-Matin* this morning, Monsieur. The

request for information. Isn't that why you are here?" I certainly hoped I'd guessed right, because my public-spirited gesture didn't seem to please him as much as one might have thought.

"You were a visitor to the Villa Mimosa? Why didn't you come forward sooner?"

"I am on holiday. I only saw the paper this morning. And that was just by chance. I'd decided to see how the bicycle race was progressing."

"Very well," said the *flic* from Monaco in the eager tone of an aficionado. "Vietto is leading. Surely a French victory this year, though look for Brambilla in the mountain stages. *Bellissimo* is Brambilla."

His companion gave him a sour look. "Why were you at the Villa Mimosa?"

"It's a long story."

"We are at your disposal, Monsieur." He sat down on the end of the bed and took out his notepad. I started with the shooting outside the gambling club and progressed to the rich, mysterious Monsieur Joubert and the even more mysterious Victor Renard, who might or might not be dead.

Inspector Chardin looked up sharply at this. "You were supposedly taking his last letter to his wife."

"Supposedly—and the letter bore that out. It was a farewell note. He had been very badly hurt, and I'm in position to know that he lost a lot of blood. His death was certainly believable, but there has been no report in the London papers. We took an interest, as you can imagine."

Inspector Chardin made a note of this. "So you did not know Monsieur Renard personally?"

"I don't believe I had ever seen him before. He was not a regular at the club."

"And Joubert?"

"I just knew him as the proprietor."

"Yet you agreed to deliver the letter for him even if it was out of your way?"

"There were inducements."

I described our bargain, and the younger man did a quick conversion from pounds to francs. "That's a lot of money for a letter."

"Too much," I agreed. "But the packet contained more than a letter."

"It would be nice to have a look at that notebook," the detective remarked when I finished describing the contents of the packet.

"Madame Renard, the Madame Renard I saw, that is, took it to the rear of the house—undoubtedly to someone else—and came back and pronounced it satisfactory."

"Then you left?"

"I left immediately. I did not want to linger at the villa, which was nearly empty of furniture and unnaturally quiet. I couldn't believe that anyone lived there, yet I had a sense that Madame Renard was not alone. For one thing, and I didn't think of this until just now, the whole house stank of cigarette smoke. I have asthma; I notice. But not Madame. I spoke to her in the doorway, and she smelled only of cologne."

"But you actually saw no one except the woman calling herself Madame Renard? As far as you know the house was otherwise empty?"

"No." I explained my detour to the tower and the two men in their blue smocks and town shoes who came out the front gate.

"Would you recognize them again?"

"Hard to say. I saw them from above. There was nothing particularly distinctive about them. One was slightly balding. Both were medium height and weight. But if the neighbors saw me, I assume they saw the men as well, perhaps more than once. And the Madame Renard that I saw—surely someone would have noticed her. She must have left at some point."

The inspector thought for a moment, letting the silence grow in the room that I now felt was distinctly warm and stuffy. He was waiting for me to tell him more, to reveal something, to betray myself. I kept my mouth shut and thought how he would look on canvas with his rather red mouth and his long yellow teeth. His fingers were stained brownish yellow, too, and he began tapping one restlessly on his knee so that I guessed he needed a smoke. Finally, he said, "There is a problem, Monsieur. A problem for you, unfortunately."

I waited; this did not sound good.

"The neighbors only report seeing you that afternoon. No one else went in or out of the Villa Mimosa that day."

I shrugged. "Perhaps they stopped peeking out their windows. Perhaps they are lying."

"Or perhaps you are, Monsieur."

"I have no reason to lie, and I had every reason to wish for Madame Renard's good health so that she could notify Joubert and erase my gambling debts."

"All this will have to be verified with our London colleagues."

I could see delays coming.

"It would be convenient if you could return with me to France. It is possible you can identify the men you claim to have seen. That would be a very strong point in your favor."

Though I pointed out that this plan would hardly be convenient for me, I was unable to convince them that I should remain in the principality. I tapped on the adjoining door, confident that Nan would have been listening, and told her that I had to return to France. She stuck her head out, glared at the two policemen, and said, "Give me your cases, dear boy. I will keep them for you."

The inspector shook his head. "It may be a few days," he said and motioned for me to collect my things and leave. Downstairs, a black car waited with a uniformed officer in the driver's seat. Inspector Chardin shook hands with his Monégasque counterpart, and I managed to wave to Arnold before I was hustled into the back of the car, the driver complaining about the weight of my cases.

"Painting supplies," I explained.

This interested the inspector. "You will help us with the picture file," he said, and after a long session with him and one of his note-taking juniors, I was seated at a big table with piles of folders and books of photographs. A resource indeed, and in a happier time, I would have enjoyed pouring over the mug shots of various French, Italian, and Corsican lowlifes. Yes, really some remarkable features but too impassive for my brush. I like extreme emotions, rage, lust, ecstasy, and I like them pictorially, too.

In any case I didn't make much progress. Only one balding man struck me as being the right type for my faux workmen. "Not him, but he was like this."

"Keep at it," Inspector Chardin ordered, and he had another book of photos brought in.

Two hours later, when I had still found nothing, he produced a couple of sheets of paper and a pencil. "You say you're a painter. Give us a sketch, then."

This certainly was my lucky day: free art work on top of hours spent in the interview room instead of lolling under the palm trees. But needs must, as the saying goes, and since I often start with a printed image, I asked for the photo that bore the closest resemblance. Normally, I paint and draw simultaneously and always with the brush. I'm not really too friendly with the pencil, and, even with the help of the photo, it took me several minutes to rough in the head. "I saw him from above, you understand."

Chardin shrugged. He breathed a melancholy resignation that I thought would have been more suited to a priest than a copper. He stood at my shoulder and watched me work. "Ah," he said when I was finished. He took the paper and disappeared with it.

On his return, he asked, "What about the other man?"

I shook my head. I had only a vague image of a square face, dark hair, heavy shoulders.

"And the girl? The one you call Madame Renard?"

I thought for a minute, trying to decide if she would be safer known or unknown to the police.

"They'll kill her, you understand," Chardin said. "When she's no longer of use to them."

I saw his point, though I wasn't entirely convinced that a Marseille street girl would be any safer in the warm embrace of the law. "Right. But I need you not to stand over me. And something to drink."

Chardin went to the door and presently I received a large glass of the local red wine. When the door was locked again, I took a clean sheet of paper and concentrated on the hallway of the Villa Mimosa with the bare walls and tile floor, and on Madame with her wide, cat's face, her small ears, and full lips. I erased once, twice, three times, and the paper took on the nasty grayish sheen of overwork before a little alteration to the brows, a change to the inside corner of one eye, a little shadow under the other and *voilà*: There she was. Though I am not fond of realism, per se, it has its moments, and this was one of them.

I got up from the bum-torturing wooden chair and went to the narrow barred window. Perhaps it was the contrast between the blue Mediterranean and the mildewed rooms of the station that depressed Inspector Chardin, who returned as I was studying the buff and sienna roofs of the town. He went right to the table and picked up the sheet. I heard him swear under his breath. "Are you sure?"

I turned around. His face had contracted with anxiety, and I wondered what I had gotten myself into. "It is as good a likeness as I can manage. It's a true impression of her."

He looked at the drawing again, shook his head, and disappeared into the hallway. When he returned, we rehashed everything I had told him, particularly about my Madame Renard, who had gone from being a no-account Marseille tart to a person of real interest.

"Did you think she was frightened?" he asked at one point.

I thought this over. "When I gave her the packet, I thought she was nervous. But when she came back to see me out, she seemed relieved. I did momentarily get the feeling she would like me to stay, but though she offered me a drink, she did not press me."

Chardin tapped the table with one long, restless finger. "This has been very helpful," he said.

I stood up like a bona fide good citizen, hoping that my passport would be returned and I would be free to go.

Chardin shook his head. "Helpful, but your story is still without corroboration. You are the only one who claims to have seen these people. You are the only one who can identify them. We must ask you to stay in the Var until further notice."

When I began to protest, he added, "With such excellent information, it will surely not be too long, Monsieur." He suggested a small and inexpensive hotel in the old part of the town, then went to the door and called for an officer to bring my cases. I was going from *en vacances* to semipermanent resident.

CHAPTER FOUR

Ah, to be *en vacances*—without money. The Hotel Phoenix was certainly cheap and the little café next door did a reasonable *sandwich au jambon*, but it did not take me more than a few days to see that I was going to have to find some means of support. Remembering the glossy young things along the *plage*, I suspected that I was now too old for my former occupation of discreet "gentleman's gentleman." With the last of the money Arnold wired me, I'd visited the casino, a bad, exciting night that emptied my pockets, and I found no business that needed my other skill, telephone operator.

I was considering various desperate measures when I remembered the "portrait artists" along the front. My drawing of the false Madame Renard had been good enough to put the wind up the

inspector. How much worse could I be than the wretched caricaturist who sat outside the casino? Remember Monet, I told myself,
who earned his pocket money doing caricatures as a boy; remember the great Daumier, who satirized the great and the corrupt! I
packed a kit, took my collapsible easel, and went to the front.

Do you think there are deep roots to one's choice of profession? I have a certain pictorial taste for pain and humiliation that
anticipate the seaside portraitist's life. One sits, one waits, one
hopes. One is rejected. One gets a client. The client is uninspiring,
the work goes badly, the client refuses to pay, perhaps a gendarme
becomes involved.

Within a few hours, I gained a new respect for the facile drafts-
man to the south of me, whose big scrawling strokes elicited wonder and whose subtle flattery disarmed the young women and their
cretinous boyfriends. A lovely liar, really. Now, I lie easily in life,
but not on canvas or paper. I find it hard to reduce a bulbous nose
or raise a low forehead or trim protruding ears even in the interests
of profit.

After eight hours in the sun, I had done three sketches, been
paid for two, and had just enough for a fish soup and a chunk of
bread; the artist's life is not always a happy one. Still, I figured things
could only get better. I set up my easel the next day within sight
of my competitor's drawings, and when I wasn't working myself, I
watched his every move.

The one great product of a neglected childhood and an irregular education is the ability to learn on the fly. Within three days, I
was turning out creditable sketches and, by dint of some shading in
charcoal, offering an alternative to the rapid pen work of my nearest competitor. I'd developed a patter, too; I can be amusing when I
want, and I really think I might have lasted the summer if I hadn't
met the Chavanel ladies.

Anastasie arrived first. She appeared out of the sun, as the pilots say, a tall, lean figure in a long black skirt, a black sunhat, sturdy heels, and a black-and-white polka-dot blouse, an ensemble from before the war, incongruous amid the bare, tanned limbs of the sun-drenched Riviera.

"Bonjour, monsieur." She tipped her head slightly, and the light caught her face, which was thin, brown, and lined like parchment. She was old and interesting, and her name was Anastasie Chavanel.

"Bonjour, madame." I made a bow to this courtly apparition.

"I see that your business is thriving." She nodded toward my metal till box.

"As much as these ever thrive," I said.

"Just so."

With modest prosperity I had acquired two folding stools. I gestured toward the client's seat and asked if Madame wished a drawing. "A portrait drawing would perhaps be more suitable than a caricature?"

She remained standing. "I have something else in mind," she said. She looked at my price list. "Thirty francs? I can offer you better than that."

This was music to my ears.

"You are, I believe, a painter?"

"My fame has preceded me." I wondered exactly how that had happened, and I couldn't help remembering that the last time an elderly lady wanted a painter, I'd spent a couple of weeks on a scaffold with extremely depressing colors.

"In a manner of speaking. Could we go somewhere to talk? This is a confidential matter."

"I am at your service." I collapsed the stools and folded up my easel, tied them together with my drawing pad and my box of pencils and charcoal, and hoisted the whole contraption on my back. I felt like Van Gogh, who did a picture of a painter burdened just so with all his equipment in the burning Provençal light.

In recompense, I anticipated a café, where she would treat me to good coffee or a glass of wine and a dish of ice cream. Instead, we took the steep hill past the *hôtel de ville* and the police station. I was sweating in the afternoon heat before we reached the top where Madame's "confidential matter" took us to a fine house in need of a great deal of money. The little garden behind the low wall and the high ironwork fence was a jungle of overgrown oleanders and mimosas, while a grove of the distinctive dark cedars of Provence shadowed the back. The windows were elegant and the door handsome, but there were loose and broken tiles on the roof, and the fine stucco work was cracked and flaking.

Inside, the hallway and the front rooms were dimmed by shutters, and I remembered the shadowed Villa Mimosa. Madame Chavanel led the way into a large square room. I expected an old lady parlor with horsehair sofas, antimacassars, tea tables, and bric-a-brac. I found a big workbench with an assortment of carpentry tools and, in the center, still smelling faintly of paint and sawdust, a large and beautifully detailed dollhouse in the very style of Madame's home—or of the Villa Mimosa, for that matter.

Though I have little interest in the miniaturist's trade, I found the small house fascinating, with what looked to be operational windows and doors and a roof of tiny tiles. "This is very impressive, Madame."

She inclined her head. "My sister and I do commissions for serious collectors. As you would imagine, everything has to be perfect."

"And so it looks." I was a little disappointed, because I could not imagine what I might add to this curious masterwork.

"One thing is missing." She touched what I'd thought was an

electric meter box and the right side wall swung open, revealing a formal parlor and, behind it, a dining room and a kitchen. As all seemed immaculately appointed, I looked at her curiously.

"Paintings," she said. "We need a small portrait here." She pointed to the wall above the fireplace where a tiny frame awaited a stamp-sized picture. "And here, on the ceiling. There will be a fresco. In oil or gouache for our purposes."

"Gods and monsters?"

"Ribbons and flowers would be better at our scale." She showed me the painting set up: two small rectangles of canvas pinned to a table easel. A large magnifying glass was mounted on a movable stand next to a container of very small red sable brushes. "As we get older, the close work is difficult. Particularly painting. We used to have a very good helper, but—times change, Monsieur."

Do they ever. I have ambitions for big paintings, for my great subject, the crucifixion, for a series of screaming heads. Now I was set to do a portrait no bigger than my thumb and a faux ceiling fresco the size of my hand. Time for some artistic temperament? I considered the heat and glare of the *plage* with its tightfisted clientele reeking of sun oil. Madame's house was cool, quiet, and dark; Madame was interesting, and, even if I weren't a gambler, I was willing to bet there was something more here than two minuscule paintings. "How much for both?"

"Could we say one hundred and fifty francs, Monsieur?"

I said we could. Madame brought me a glass of white wine, cold and clear, accompanied by a plate of biscuits. We discussed the colors of the fresco, which seemed to be her primary concern, and I began work. The "fresco" was to be in a fat oval. A bouquet of roses and lavender in the center, a wreath of oleander, bay, and rosemary around the edges. "The herbs of Provence," Madame said. The colors would be soft, faintly dusty.

"Distemper or gouache would be ideal," I said, "but not as lasting as oil."

"Oils as dry as you can make them, then." She opened one shutter to give me better light and left the room. When she returned three hours later, the white hot light was sliding to gold, and I knew that the colors would begin to deceive me.

Madame took the magnifying glass from its stand and examined the ceiling design carefully. "Very nice, Monsieur. A few days to dry and it can be pasted in place. Very good."

"The portrait's roughed in, but it will need to dry before I can add the features. Tomorrow, perhaps?"

"And a little blue," she said. "At the neck. To pick up the colors of the chairs."

I took my brush and added a ribbon trim.

"You are a discovery, Monsieur." She gave me one hundred francs, the balance to be due when I finished the portrait, then asked, "You will stay for dinner? My sister and I so rarely have the pleasure of company."

The smell of good things issuing from the back of the house reminded me that I hadn't seen a decent meal in days. I said that I would like that very much.

"Indeed you will," she said. "My sister is a wonderful cook."

That was an understatement. An hour later we sat down to a fine bouillabaisse with good bread and tomatoes and olives, served up in the stone-floored kitchen by Agathe Chavanel, who was as plump and jolly as her sister was thin and serious. She had bright, protuberant blue eyes, and the strong Chavanel features were padded out with folds of soft, fair skin like a pug dog's. She padded around in espadrilles, wore a big white apron even at table, and seemed in every way a less formal personality than her sister.

Both of them were very complimentary about my efforts for the dollhouse. They wanted to know how I had come to speak such excellent French and how my holiday had been. It was all very pleasant, the good food enhanced for me by the old-fashioned table, sideboard, and storage cupboards. Even the battered easy chairs by the fire reminded me of the Irish kitchens of my youth where I spent so much time with Nan. Delightful, really, but I couldn't help noticing the glances that passed between the two old ladies. They had clearly lived together long enough to need few words, and I sensed another conversation progressing beneath my account of our adventures at the tables in Monte Carlo or of the rebuilding going on at Dieppe's port.

"You've seen the length of France," Agathe said when the dinner plates had been cleared away, and we were eating grapes with little layered cakes covered in chocolate. She leaned forward slightly.

"And now you are here," said her sister. "Without your friends and without work."

"I've had the misfortune of helping the police."

"I knew it," said Anastasie to her sister. "I said it had to be him, did I not?"

Agathe nodded her head. "My sister is an excellent judge of character. How many times we have relied on her instinct!"

"And now?" Anastasie asked her.

"I think so," said Agathe, before turning to me. "If you are telling the truth about the police, that is. Can you tell us why you are assisting them?"

"The killing at the Villa Mimosa. I was apparently the last visitor."

They both crossed themselves, and Anastasie said, "You saw her, then."

"No. I saw another, much younger woman who claimed to be Madame Renard but was not."

"She is the one we are interested in," said Agathe. "Please tell us everything you can remember."

I hesitated. If my loyalties lay anywhere, they lay with the young woman who'd been "down on her luck," as Arnold so tactfully phrased it, and who was living by her wits as I had done at about the same age. "Could I ask why you are interested?"

Now it was their turn to think things over. Agathe decided. She went to a large, carved wooden bureau with a fine collection of framed photographs. I only then noticed that half a dozen of them had been turned to face the wall. "If you can describe her to us, we will explain everything."

I repeated the description I'd given the police: the wide face, the alert expression, the short blond hair.

"Blond?" the old ladies asked in unison.

"Most likely dyed," I said.

"But short. Her hair was short?"

I drew a line halfway down my neck. "About to here. And she's a few inches shorter than me. Thin. She could do with a meal like this," I added and immediately regretted it when I saw that this idea hurt them.

Agathe held out the photograph. "Was this her?"

Small, slim, dark, wide face, a longish nose, which I realized that I had gotten wrong in my drawing, a nose that might one day take her features from appealing to distinguished. Her hair was long and looked almost black. Very like, but identical? This was a girl, no more than fourteen or fifteen, and I wasn't sure, until Anastasia brought me another photo and this time there was no doubt. "Yes, that's her. Who is she?"

Before answering, Agathe rose and turned all the photos of the young woman so that they faced the room. "We did not want to confuse your memory," she said. "This is our niece, Cybèle. Our late sister's child."

"Our daughter, almost," said Anastasie. "We raised her from the time she was ten."

"But she hasn't been living here?"

"She disappeared right at the end of the war," Agathe said. "It's been over two years."

"She looks to be in good health," I said. I did not feel I should speculate on her survival skills.

"We blame ourselves," said Anastasie. "If we had been more strict immediately."

"If, if, if," said Agathe. "It suited us at the time."

Her sister's face froze. She had been moving around the room, an energetic, angular woman of indeterminate age. Now she sat down and looked old. After a moment, she said, "Cybèle was a delightful child. Very happy, very kind. One of those people who see the best in others."

"Making her," said Agathe, "wonderful company but maybe not fitting her for life as it is. Especially in wartime."

"She fell in love with a young soldier. She was just seventeen."

"He was nice enough," Agathe added. "He was just a boy himself."

"Eighteen, I think. The Wehrmacht was sending out very young troops by then."

I could see the shape of the story already; it's as old as Romeo and Juliet, and it tends to end badly. As hers did.

"He left right after the landings. He promised her he'd come back." Anastasie shrugged and raised her hands with one of those inimitable French gestures that express a wealth of worldly knowledge.

"He might have died the day after he left," Agathe said. "He was just a boy. They had little transport and the Maquis was fighting all through the hills."

"She was set to wait for him."

"You understand, we thought she would be safe with us," Agathe interrupted in an anguished tone. "We thought that our war record would protect her."

"But there were, Monsieur, various thugs in patriotic disguise. Do you know the type?"

I did.

"Who were keen to cover their own dubious activities by denouncing others. Young women, especially, who could be shamed for 'horizontal collaboration,' while the black marketers and the real Vichy types went on to power or wealth."

"Or both," said Agathe.

"One day in the square, she had her head shaved, her clothes torn off. We were too late to stop it."

"We might not have been able to stop it," Agathe said.

"We should have stopped it all sooner," Anastasie said. "When she first became interested in him."

"But it suited us." I realized that the jolly Agathe was perhaps the more ruthless of the two.

"In what way, Madame?"

"What better cover, Monsieur, for a clandestine operation than to have a visiting German soldier?"

"It was a fatal error," said Anastasie.

"We survived," her sister said, "and Cybèle, too, when many others were rounded up and shot."

"She survived to have her heart broken and her name smeared. This is a small town, Monsieur. She packed her bag and disappeared within days. We have not heard from her since."

"I'm sorry that I can't tell you more. As I told the police, I saw two men leave the villa, but I did not linger after they left, and I did not see her leave. I know nothing more, though the *flics* seem to think I do."

There was a long silence at this. Agathe passed around a bottle of dessert wine and little glasses. The kitchen clock ticked loudly and a tap dripped in counterpoint.

"Why did you go to the Villa Mimosa?" Anastasie asked at last.

"I was delivering a package from Victor Renard, who was supposedly dead."

"It would be hard for Victor Renard to be dead," Anastasie said, "given that he never existed."

"I saw him shot. In London. His blood ruined my shirt."

"Whoever was shot was not Monsieur Renard," Anastasie said firmly. "During the war, 'Monsieur Renard' was a password. People looking for assistance would ask for him. If they looked all right, we helped them. If not, 'Monsieur Renard' was away on business."

"At that time we were still very skilled in fine work," Agathe added, seeing that I looked puzzled. "There were many people with unsatisfactory papers, refugees, Jews, known Communists."

"Or no papers at all," said Anastasie. "We would make such 'corrections' and additions as was necessary."

"That must have been dangerous—and perhaps lucrative?" I was thinking of the list of names, of the fact that a man had been shot and a woman murdered for it.

"We did not do it for the money," Anastasie said, "but we had to survive, and the market for our work had collapsed. We worked on a barter system: documents for jewelry, antiques, pictures, which we sold to the Germans, who had a great appetite for such things."

I could see complications on every side, and I began to suspect that these two charmers had played every angle possible. Survival demands a certain moral flexibility, but they didn't mention when— or if—they'd ended their business with the papers, and I wondered how many lowlifes had wanted new documents when the Allies invaded. "Why would the people in the villa use the Renard name?"

"I do not know, Monsieur. I do not know what was in the package you delivered. We hope"—and here she turned to glance at Agathe— "that it was Cybèle's idea. That it was a little message to us."

"An expensive message, Madame."

Again the two women exchanged glances. "We have a proposition, Monsieur," said Agathe. "Your work with the pictures is excellent, but we have another job we'd like you to undertake."

I waited.

"We want you to find Cybèle." She held up her hand to stop me from speaking. "You can go places that we cannot, at least not inconspicuously. A young man asking questions about a young woman, well, that is natural, is it not? While two old ladies in certain places would raise questions right away."

"I would like to help you and Mademoiselle Cybèle, too, but it is a police matter. I'm guessing that you have contact with Inspector Chardin, that he told you about me and showed you my drawing. Can't you leave this in his hands?"

"The inspector is very decent," Agathe said, "but Cybèle is an adult. Because she left of her own free will, the police will not devote too much time to her disappearance."

"And then, there is incident at the Villa Mimosa." Anastasie pronounced "incident" with distaste. "It might be better if Cybèle were not found just now by the police."

"Granted, but you need a professional investigator, someone who is skilled in these matters and who knows the area."

"The area may be larger than you think," Anastasie said. "This started in London."

"That's all moot. I'm afraid that without my passport I am confined to town. I have no identification of any kind."

Agathe snorted. "Set your mind at rest on that score, Monsieur. An identity card is simplicity itself."

I had visions of Monte Carlo, Nice, and Paris, and I thought that even a passport might not be beyond their expertise. At the very least, I could drink with their money in every café and bistro on the Riviera. I was within a hairsbreadth of accepting when something about Anastasie's gaunt features reminded me of Nan. I have a weakness for old ladies, especially ones who are dubious, and I shook my head. "Do not tempt me, Madame. I have no competence in this area, and I would only be taking your money under false pretenses."

Though they implored me to think it over and their obvious desperation made them persuasive, I resisted admirably. I left in the unfamiliar aura of virtue, my portrait kit on my back, and promised to return the next afternoon to finish up the tiny pictures for the dollhouse.

CHAPTER FIVE

I could see the glowing windows of the casino and the streetlights wavering behind the palm trees along the front. Now and again the night breeze brought a snatch of music, but in the upper town, where people worked for a living, the streets were dark, the little squares deserted. Not that I mind darkness. Compared to the total blackout during the war, even the shadowed alleys and the black pools beneath the lime trees were easily navigated. I'm a "chimes at midnight" fellow in any case, and when I saw a tiny café with its string of colored lights still burning, I went in for a few drinks. With money in my pocket, I was up for adventures of one sort or another, but the room was nearly deserted. The few fellows leaning against the zinc all seemed preoccupied with the cares of the world.

Unable to draw them out, I turned my mind unwillingly to the old ladies and to the proposition that I had rejected.

Certainly Anastasie and Agathe had charm, but their activities during the war opened numerous possibilities, mostly doubtful. After my second cognac, it came to me that I was out after hours on the home turf of my friends from the Villa Mimosa. Considering that I had been on the front every day for a week, advertising my services, anyone interested would have a pretty good idea of how to find me.

A foolish thought. Turn it the other way: I'd been out on the front, sketching the holidaymakers for a week without trouble. The men from the Villa Mimosa were doubtless long gone and the old ladies' niece with them. Thinking good riddance to all of them, I tipped the barman and set off for the hotel via the long flight of stairs that led to the fresh vegetable market with its dark rows of stalls and tables. Once across the street under the rail bridge, I'd be in the shopping district within a block of the front and the cheerful faces of the late-night cafés and bistros.

I had just reached the sidewalk that ran past the market when there was a sound behind me, and I was struck in the back with enormous force. Overbalanced by my easel and painting equipment, I stumbled onto my knees, scuffing my hands on the paving. The man behind me began swearing, as if this was an outrageous deviation from some obscure plan, and tried to tear the easel from my back. While he was struggling to part me from my livelihood, the folding stools came loose from the bundle. I got to my feet with one of the sturdy wood and canvas frames in hand and swung it at his head.

It cracked his shoulder, instead, and he struck at my face. Another blow and another, and I realized that he was too big and too strong for me. He grabbed the shoulder strap that secured my painting gear and set to pound me unconscious. Desperate, I gave up trying to clobber him with the stool and thrust it at close range into his groin. He released me with a roar. I swung the wooden stool as hard as I could into his knee, then turned and ran. With his heavy and uneven tread behind me, I raced toward the rail bridge. Once in the shadow of the abutment, I ducked down an alley behind the station cafés and found my way past garbage bins and loading docks to the lights of the esplanade.

I had almost reached the casino before I realized that my pursuer had vanished. Sore and breathless, I sat down on one of the benches along the *plage*. My face was wet; when I rubbed it, my hand looked dark. A moment's investigation revealed that both my nose and my lip were bleeding, and I could feel my right eye beginning to swell. But if my beauty was compromised, I was otherwise unhurt, and I went to a nearby fountain to wash my face and clean my shirt.

I unhooked my now-depleted bundle of equipment, laid it on the ground, and splashed in the cool water. I was standing there, the cuts on my face stinging, when I noticed my folding easel. Suddenly what had been an inconvenience of the midnight hour took on a different coloration. Stuck in the middle of the box that holds my pencils and colors was the hilt of a knife. I reached for it and gave a tug without success. No wonder my assailant had been annoyed. After several tries, I put my foot on the easel and levered the knife out, splintering the wood.

I was still considering the implications when voices drifted along from the casino. It wouldn't do to be found bleeding with a good-sized knife in my hand. I slipped the weapon inside the easel box and hoisted what was left of my painting kit onto my shoulder. Keeping to well-lighted streets, I made my way back to the Hotel Phoenix, where with the barest nod to the concierge, I got into the little iron elevator and was hoisted up to bed.

In the morning, I faced decisions. I looked as if I'd been run

over by a truck and, though I am skillful with makeup, day-
light hours would inevitably reveal the damage. Then there was
the knife, big, sharp, and serious, one of the many military and
quasi-military weapons floating about. It suggested a quick exit
from town.

The simplest way would be to retrieve my passport. With what
I'd earned from the Chavanel ladies, I could make my way north
and take the ferry home if I had documents. After fending off questions and concerns from the concierge and consuming more than
my share of bread and hot chocolate, I presented my case to Inspector Chardin, who roused himself from his melancholy to greet me
with all the false geniality of officialdom. Ignoring my battered face,
he peppered me with irrelevant questions: Was I enjoying my stay
in their so charming town? The wonderful sand beach, the historic
associations, the notable domestic architecture? He sounded more
like a civic booster than a copper.

"If one can enjoy the precarious living of the beachfront artist," I said.

"Ah, Monsieur, a man of your talents will make his way." And
he gave me a shrewd look as if he knew that I'd been in touch with
the Chavanels.

"It was tolerable until last night," I said. I opened my painting box and took out the knife. I laid it on his desk and turned
the box to show him how my assailant had splintered the wood.
"I want out, Inspector. I have done nothing but deliver a package for an acquaintance, and now I have nearly been murdered
on the street. My painting equipment has been damaged or lost,
and with it, my livelihood. I want to return home, and I want
my passport."

The inspector expressed proper concern about this, had my
statement taken, and went over with me not once but twice the cir-

cumstances of the attack. This was a serious matter, he assured me, especially in light of recent events. But, as he put it, I surely saw that it was even more important than ever that I be "on hand"?

I certainly did not. I had money for train fare and I said, "I'll go to our consulate in Nice. I'll make a formal complaint."

"I wouldn't do that," said Chardin. "We need you here and we have the means of keeping you here."

I didn't like this at all.

"We have observed your habits," he said. "And while we do not have all the Anglo-Saxon prejudices, we can always find a charge under the somewhat elastic public indecency laws. Such a charge would not help you with your consul."

I was tempted to tell him just what I thought about these maneuvers. But that would be to tip my hand. With a restrained dignity not at all natural to me, I expressed my disappointment at the perfidy of the French police, collected my shattered gear, and left. I went back to the hotel, painted until lunchtime, then made a circuitous way to the Chavanels' villa.

"Monsieur!" Anastasie exclaimed when she opened the door. "What has happened?"

"I've reconsidered your offer," I said.

"Agathe! Agathe!" she called and led me into the kitchen, where I was plied with herbal tea and bread and, more restorative than either, a shot of cognac, as I recounted my adventures of the night before and my meeting with Inspector Chardin.

Agathe shook her head at this.

"There was a chance I could retrieve my passport."

"You are lucky to be out and about," she said. "For a variety of reasons, they want to solve this soon."

"So he gave me to understand. I want out and I want to purchase a passport."

"Passports are no longer for sale," Anastasie said. "A *carte d'identité* is another matter, but strictly by barter as we have discussed."

I thought this over. The chances of my finding the girl were not good at all, but their willingness to drive a hard bargain was hardly my fault. "If I can find Cybèle," I said, "you will make me a passport. Just good enough to get onto the Channel ferry."

They exchanged looks before Anastasie nodded. "Though if you find Cybèle, I think you will be able to clear yourself."

"Either way," I said. "I need to get home; I need peace and quiet to paint."

"Which reminds us," Agathe said, and they set me to work on the little portrait. When I was finished, we had a fine lunch and the old ladies gave me as much information as they could about Cybèle. The girl was musical, it turned out, a fine singer and a respectable dancer. "Too inexperienced for the stage," Agathe said, "but clubs, cafés, we think she could work those."

I thought about that. It was possible that "Madame Renard's" underfed look was from dancing and that the girl's sharp manner and cynical expression had been honed in the smoky dives that are the lot of friendless beginners. I'd figured the streets, but from what the old ladies were telling me, their niece was an intelligent and talented girl and, as they put it, "nobody's fool."

"Except in romance," I suggested.

"She grew up fast," Anastasie said abruptly. "We think Nice more likely than Marseille."

"Any reason?"

"We used to visit relatives there—before '43, of course. Once the Italians moved in, that was out of bounds."

I wondered about that or if their contacts in the Fascist territory had proved useful. "And who are these relatives?"

"They died during the war, the bombardment, the famine. But

Cybèle knew the town, and she may have contacted people who knew her cousins. Jerome Chavanel was a waiter at the Hotel Negresco. He would have had good contacts at restaurants, nightclubs, cafés."

"When did he die?"

"In '44."

"I'll start by asking for him. Did you have any contact with her at all after she left?"

"A postcard only. She'd gone to Antibes. She had a friend there, a potter named Suzanne. I don't know her last name."

Anastasie shook her head, as if she only now realized how thin this information was and how unlikely success would be for even a skilled investigator familiar with the territory. "It's not very much," she said.

But Antibes was the magic word. I had read that Picasso was working near there, and without any real desire to meet the painter who had impressed me so much, I found a strong impulse to see the area where he worked. "Get me the identity card and a little money and I will do my best," I said.

We shook hands formally and they promised the card for later that afternoon. I walked back to the hotel to pack my bag and my painting kit, stopping for a farewell drink at the café I'd been frequenting. I had barely settled under one of its umbrellas when a stout fellow with dark jowls and the face of a lesser emperor sat down heavily in the seat opposite me. He took out a handkerchief and wiped his face.

I waited. As a romantic approach, this lacked something in subtlety. He signaled for Louis, who brought us a carafe of white wine and some biscuits. All very civilized.

"To your good health," my companion said when the drinks were poured. Despite his heavy, even brutal, appearance, his voice was soft and insinuating. "May it continue."

First a knife in the back and now a toast to my health. I said nothing.

He took a drink of his wine, held it up to the light, took another sip. He helped himself to three of the biscuits at once and said, "Monsieur Joubert is very displeased."

"You're from Joubert? Where are my gambling chits? No, no," I said when he began describing his master's wrath. "I got a package from Joubert. I delivered the package. I have had nothing but trouble since."

"You delivered it to the wrong woman after alerting half the town."

"I was given no directions and no description of the lady in question. Joubert is an incompetent ass. You can remind him that I have a signed agreement for a job that I have completed."

"You are behaving very foolishly. You are broke and without papers—that is correct? The police have your passport?"

"My problems are nothing to you."

"You are broke in a foreign country without documents. You need me, Monsieur."

I said several rude things about my needs of the moment, but my fat, vaguely sinister visitor was undeterred. "You have, moreover, friends in England. Friends who are known to Monsieur Joubert. It is in their interest as well as yours that you cooperate."

I didn't like this at all. I would have to wire Arnold, make arrangements for Nan. "If Joubert wants some caricatures from the beachfront, I'll be happy to oblige. Otherwise, you can tell him, he's out of luck."

"Monsieur Joubert wants that package back. You are to get it for him."

"Oh, right, without papers, without money, without knowing what is going on."

He put a fat envelope on the table. "A little walking-around money," he said.

I didn't touch it. "Walking around here has not been entirely pleasant."

"Hence this small gratuity. You and Monsieur Joubert have enemies in common. They have his package."

"And they'd like me dead. Excuse me if I'd rather avoid them."

"Monsieur Joubert wants to retrieve that package. See it happens," he said, getting awkwardly to his feet. "Otherwise, I can't vouch for the health of either you or your friends."

Being *en vacances* was gaining new meaning all the time.

I wired a warning to Arnold and rethought my plan—a simple, touristy plan, I now realized—of storing my painting kit in left luggage and taking the train to Nice. Neither would do at all. I had to assume the police or my emissary from Joubert or even my assailant of last night would be keeping an eye on the *gare*. I would have to find an alternate route. I ruffled through the bills in the envelope and put them in my wallet. At this juncture, trapped like the proverbial rat, et cetera, et cetera, I thought a night on the town would be a good idea, and, under the pressure of imminent violent death, I came up with a possible companion.

CHAPTER SIX

The sun slid down into the Mediterranean, the dark sea of Homer and of Aeschylus, whom I love. Because I was both badly and briefly educated, the great Greek poets were never ruined for me with classes and exams. Especially near nightfall, the time when blood is shed in the palaces, the time secrets are unfolded and rituals begin, I often think of the Greeks, my spiritual mentors. After a time of war and misery, they were distractingly vivid to my imagination—which, I reminded myself, must be redirected to finding my way through the town's narrow streets, all seemingly deserted except for some lurking cats and a small dog barking behind an iron fence.

Had there been a patisserie on the corner? A laundry? I couldn't remember and I didn't want to ask. With night coming on, the shadows of the stone walls started to remind me less of ancient kings and more of local thugs. My bag was a nuisance, too, but if I was to troll the various clubs and cafés of Nice, I needed a dinner jacket and a pair of decent shoes. Another little alley. I'd come down toward the sea again, and I could see the coastal road that I'd last glimpsed from the sidecar of Pierre's motorcycle. Head west again, remember the turns. Yes, there was the *boulangerie*, and there was the sign: BICYCLETTES. My prospects brightened slightly when I saw the black motorcycle with its fishlike and uncomfortable sidecar waiting in front.

I set down my case and listened. The showroom was dark but the big metal doors of the garage were open and the interior lit. Voices? No. Just the soft clinks of gears being adjusted and the shush of tires being inflated. I walked across the yard, stuck my case behind a trash barrel, and went to the door. Pierre's curly head—another little echo of the Greeks—was bent over a derailleur. He was moving the pedals by hand and fiddling with the shifting.

"*Bon soir.*" He straightened up with a start, as handsome as I remembered, even without his memorable cycling kit. "Sorry," I said in French, "I didn't mean to startle you."

"Monsieur Francis."

"The same. Preserved thanks to your kindness."

He looked shamefaced and uneasy.

"We had such a pleasant evening. I wondered if you might like to go to dinner."

"Ah, Monsieur," he gestured toward the shop, the bicycles.

"One must eat." I could see that there were several bicycles finished and ready with their bills attached. He was not busy; he was embarrassed, and so he should be. As a matter of principle, I avoid assisting the police, but how could I reproach him when I was, myself, a prisoner of the Riviera, "helping with police inquiries"?

But perhaps not for long, if I could exert my charm. "I can offer you Cannes. A very good restaurant. We begin with a pâté and a salad. A dry wine. We progress to mussels with garlic with, I think, a white Burgundy. And for dessert, I favor a selection of small tarts and some Sauternes."

He was tempted. Of course, he was. France had food, but food was expensive and every other person was hungry. Postwar, cuisine, high and low, was on everyone's mind.

"Cannes has some fine restaurants," he said. "But pricey."

"I have come into a little money. As an indirect result of being questioned by the police."

"Rare good fortune, Monsieur," he said, and I thought he relaxed a little.

"Don't feel bad about *les flics*," I said. "If not you, the hotel concierge or the café waiters or some busybody on the front would have pointed me out. You're a good citizen, and I'm in a pickle but not in any real trouble."

"We'd been seen at the restaurant," he said quickly. "They said you were a witness to the killing."

"If that were true, I'd be dead. I delivered a package to the house just about an hour before you gave me a lift. I suspect the victim was already dead when I arrived that afternoon."

"Oh, very certainly, Monsieur. Very certainly."

This put my situation in a new light. "How can you be sure?"

"The smell, of course. The neighbors went to investigate early the next morning."

I swore under my breath at Inspector Chardin. "But they told the police they saw no one but me. That can't have been true. Two men followed me from the villa. If the neighbors saw me, they almost certainly saw the men leave, too."

"They are frightened, Monsieur. Everyone is frightened, not of those particular men, but of their employer, who was very big during the war. Very big. Official, almost. People remember."

"So the men were known. And known also to the police?"

"How could they not be, Monsieur?"

How indeed! A little more of this and I'd be "down the rabbit hole," as my depraved uncle Lastings of affectionate memory used to say. But more than ever, I needed to get out of town, and my escort seemed hesitant. *Take the bull by the horns*, my nan whispered. "Would you know a good restaurant in Cannes?" I asked.

When he nodded, I pulled out a roll of Joubert's francs. I handed them over and said, "Treat me to dinner."

He ruffled through the bills and raised an eyebrow. "You mentioned mussels," he said with the fussy precision of the gourmet, "but I rather fancy a fricassee of rabbit or a veal escalope."

"Either would be delightful with a fish soup to start."

He put the bills in his pocket. "With perhaps a small pizza with olives?"

"The very thing."

"And I think a *mousse au chocolat* for dessert." He went to a hook behind the bench and collected a key.

"I might lean to *crème brûlée*, myself."

"Some of each," Pierre said decisively. He tossed me a pair of biker's goggles. "My cousin has a restaurant in Cannes. Not fancy but excellent, Monsieur."

"Call me Francis; I am in your hands entirely." A figure of speech suggesting the delightful prospects that my charms might accomplish.

He switched off the lights and locked up the garage. I thought he might balk when he saw my bag, a small carpet valise borrowed from the Chavanel ladies, but I squeezed into the sidecar before he could protest, and after a moment's hesitation he went back for a rope, lashed the bag to the cycle proper, and hopped on the machine. "Hang on, Francis," he said. With a bump and a rumble we rolled onto the street and down the hill to where the sea was a blackness broken only by the lights of distant boats.

Once on the corniche road, Pierre gunned the engine. Coming in, without goggles, blinded by dust and grit, and tortured by loose bike parts, had been misery. With vision and comfort, this was different. We roared east, flat out on the straights, trusting physics to keep us on the curves, slowing a fraction for the lights of the little fishing hamlets, then rocketing off into the darkness. The hills rose black above us, the sea dropped away into eternity, and we raced between them, almost drunk with exhilaration. Here was what I'd glimpsed on canvas, the dissolution of the world into dark energy. I started whooping with joy, and over the sound of the engine, Pierre shouted menu suggestions and detailed a wine list of ever-increasing complexity.

We reached the bay at Cannes almost too soon. We shot along the wide curving beach, past the lights of the waterfront cafés and hotels, and up to a small bright restaurant with candlelit tables under the umbrellas and, inside, a cheerful bar decorated with pictures of football and bicycle teams. Pierre was embraced; my hand was shaken. Pierre consulted with the head waiter and the chef, before we were led to a sidewalk table. A carafe of the local white appeared and a basket of good bread.

"*Bonne chance* with your race," I said.

"And to your venture, whatever it is."

I'd need all the luck I could get, but I believe in putting pleasure before business. We had soup, we had pizza, we had fish and veal and beans and lovely fried potatoes. We had three bottles of wine and more desserts than were good for us, and afterward we walked barefoot along the sand, an unaccustomed activity that shows just how besotted I was with Pierre.

When I suggested that we should take a room, that it was not safe for him to ride back, he agreed, and that turned out lovely, too. I'd say a fine evening in every way, and as evening turned into the next morning, it became profitable, for thanks to Joubert's money and that fine dinner, I learned some interesting things, even a possible identity for Victor Renard, the man who never was. This was in the wee hours of the morning, when Pierre went out onto the tiny balcony of the room to smoke.

The moment was right, and I asked, "So who owns the Villa Mimosa?"

I saw his shoulders move. "It *was* owned by Paul Desmarais, who was a trucker. During the war, he made a killing in the black market and bought the villa. He'd been a poor man but a very good mechanic, very ingenious. We had little or no gasoline, you understand, Francis. Trucks, cars, buses, whatever, had to be converted to run on charcoal or some other fuel. Desmarais could drive trucks and keep them running. He was shrewd and ruthless and he saw an opportunity."

"To get rich."

"To get very rich." Pierre paused again. "Soon he had money and connections. He cultivated everyone who might be useful, made loans to businesses, helped with dodgy papers."

I thought about the Chavanels. And also about Pierre's little bicycle repair shop and store. He was young to own even a small business, and I thought I must tread carefully. "Many must have done the same," I suggested. "The black market was extensive, yes?"

"And essential to our survival. No one liked it, but no one held that too much against him."

"We made some compromises on our side of the water, too," I said.

"Desmarais had opportunities you English lacked. When the Germans came in '43, he got himself into the Milice."

"The Milice?"

"A right-wing Fascist paramilitary. Pro-Vichy, as opposed to the Cagoule, which was right-wing and Fascist and all the rest but anti-Vichy and anti-German."

"French politics are bizarrely complex."

"Politics are a load of shit," said Pierre, and he was silent for a while.

"His work during the war frightened the Villa Mimosa neighbors."

"It certainly did. The men you saw worked for him. They protected his trucks, first. Then they were muscle for the Milice, protecting collaborators, torturing and killing resisters, hunting down Jews and refugees. A month or so ago, they showed up again at the villa. Are they still working for him? Nobody knows. But people are still afraid."

"Desmarais has disappeared," I guessed.

"Yes."

"Recently?" I was thinking of Victor Renard, who might or might not be dead in London.

"No, no. When the Allies landed—our town had the honor as you may know, Francis—the Milice fled with the Germans into the hills. They went up, the Maquis came down; men with guns everywhere. Scores were settled. But Desmarais ditched his Milice uniform and put his trucks at the service of the Americans. You see how smart he is?"

"They knew nothing about him, whereas the Free French—"

"Exactly. Next thing you know, he's advising the Yanks and running supplies and his shit smells sweeter than ever."

"A piece of work. Eventually, they must have gotten wise to him."

"At that point, Desmarais took his money and scrammed. Some said he went to South America, some said he went to Spain. Or Germany."

"Or London?"

The tip of the cigarette glowed red. "London, possibly. He could have gotten papers. Perhaps he even got some from the Americans. He made himself very useful," Pierre said and fell silent.

A few minutes later I asked him if he knew the murdered woman's real identity.

"No. She was not local. The villa was empty until just recently. I train up that way. You've got to do the hills to get your legs in shape."

He elaborated on the masochistic rituals of the serious cyclist: hills and more hills, brutal climbs and suicidal descents. I was afraid that remembering so much exertion and misery might put the Villa Mimosa out of his mind, but, no. He'd seen a car and then a truck parked out front.

"Did you see the girl, the thin blonde who was pretending to be Madame Renard?"

"No. I saw an older woman who I assumed had rented—or bought—the place. I saw her once or twice. A car would be parked there, a fine Peugeot sedan. Never for very long. I'd see it maybe on my way out but not on my way back. I stopped to admire it one day, and she came out like she was expecting someone."

She had been expecting me, I realized, or someone else dispatched from Joubert.

"Did she say anything?"

"I complimented her on the car. She agreed it was a fine one." His cigarette glowed in the darkness. "How strange to think that she had only days to live. Maybe not even that long."

"Why do you say that?"

"I heard that the body had been kept for some time."

This was a disagreeable thought, though, if true, it surely put me beyond suspicion. "In this climate?"

He took another drag of the cigarette. "We have to keep our

fish cold. There are many facilities with refrigeration and ice. Not impossible."

"So my Madame Renard might have known nothing about the murder." I really hoped that.

"If she's smart, she knows nothing and forgets even that."

"I'm wondering if she might be local," I said cautiously. Pierre was special, but who knew what his politics were—or had been—and what he might feel about the Chavanel ladies. "Thin, pretty, short dyed blond hair, no older than you. She looked like a dancer. I thought maybe an entertainer of some sort. Sound like anyone you'd remember?"

"The only dancer I know was dark, black hair, black eyes." He spoke almost too quickly and dismissively.

"Hair can be bleached. For professional reasons."

"Possible," he said, but if he knew more or guessed which way my interest ran, he did not say. His cigarette arched away into the shadows, and he came back to bed, putting questions quite out of my mind but starting the day in a highly satisfactory manner.

Sunup and both of us hungover with various excesses, Pierre dropped me at the station. "A fine dinner," he said. "A fine evening."

"If I can come into money, we must do it again. Perhaps at the bike race."

"In eight days, then."

"How will I find you?"

"Look for the support cars for our regional team, Southeast France. You'll see our colors. *Allez la Sud-Est!*"

"*Allez la Sud-Est!*" I repeated.

He paused as if he wanted to say something more, and perhaps he would have, but the express was called for Nice, Menton, Ventimiglia. I gave him a hug and started for the platform.

"Francis."

I turned for a last look at him, standing straight and handsome, the early sun lightening his thick, curly hair.

"Be careful," he called. "Remember our politics are strange, and you are a stranger here."

CHAPTER SEVEN

I had a lot to think about in the train. For one thing, there were my brand-new papers and my brand-new name, trifles in my sea of troubles, but easier to obsess about first thing in the morning than armed bully boys. Though I'd never much fancied the name, "Marcel," I must now think of Proust and make my way through life as Marcel Lepage, furniture refinisher and decorator. I hoped said Marcel could stay clear of the glum, and probably corrupt, Inspector Chardin, who had detained me for reasons that seemed increasingly mysterious.

Of course, my new cognomen came courtesy of the charming old Chavanels, which led me direct to another source of anxiety, since they might well have had connections to Desmarais during the war. If so, I guessed they would have a much better chance of locating their niece than I ever would, and what their game was with me, I couldn't begin to guess. Even Pierre, with his splendid back and magnificent legs, was not safe for contemplation. He had told me a good deal but I guessed that he knew more.

With all these considerations, I was well on my way to radical skepticism by the time we rattled into the belle epoque station at Nice, with its high glass canopy and fine ironwork, so airy, so elegant, so redolent of leisure and light. Being a creature of darkness, myself, I concluded that the faster I located Cybèle Chavanel, got a passport, and left the splendors of the Riviera, the better I'd be.

Eight a.m. Too early for clubs to be open or nightlife to be awake. I stashed my valise in left luggage and set out in the morning air, perfumed with the smell of the newly washed sidewalks, sea salt, and uncertain drains. My destination was the Hotel Negresco, where the Chavanels' cousin, assuming there ever was such a person, had worked. As soon as I reached the palm-lined Promenade des Anglais, I spotted the enormous pile, topped by a vast pink Easter egg dome with "Hotel Negresco" in huge letters stretched across the front.

One look was enough. The doorman, as grand as an admiral, the mile-high windows, the ornate balconies, the splendid plantings, and the superb view of the aquamarine sea told me that unless I broke the bank at Monte Carlo, I wouldn't pass muster as a guest. Not for the first time, I missed Arnold, who travels with an air of bourgeois rectitude and is always deemed acceptable, even with such as me in tow.

Fortunately, my rackety early existence in Berlin and Paris taught me a number of useful skills. I made my way to the rear of the establishment where I knew that the cooks would already be well into a long day. Dining room and room service breakfasts would be going up, and that meant dishes coming down—sometimes literally, by the sounds issuing from the kitchen. I reached the doors in time to catch a florid bouquet of French profanity, followed by another crash, shouts, and banging doors. Oblivious to all this, a thin sous-chef with a white toque and a long white apron stood smoking on the step. He looked sallow and overworked, but the light eyes in his long, bony face were shrewd.

"A busy morning," I said.

"Shorthanded as usual. The tourists stay for the summer now, but the hotel lets the extra winter staff go."

An opportunity for Monsieur Lepage. "Perhaps you could do with some assistance with the dishes."

He shrugged and looked me over. "Work in a kitchen before?"

"Dishwasher," I said, which, sadly, was true. "And some catering." This was not true, unless helping with sandwiches for my wartime ARP post counted.

"A day or two would be all," he said. "There will be friends of friends interested."

"Ideal. I find myself temporarily embarrassed." This was Marcel talking. I am almost never embarrassed, but Monsieur Lepage was a different item. "A run of bad luck."

"Better temporarily than permanently," said the sous-chef. He carefully extinguished his cigarette and tucked the butt in his pocket before ushering me into the kitchen, a maelstrom of sweaty line cooks and dishwashers, of white-coated waiters demanding croissants and pots of chocolate and English breakfasts and plates of cheese and fresh fruit. The staff squeezed between racks of clean dishes and of breakfast trays set up and waiting for their entrées; they dodged stoves with huge burners throwing out hellish heat, and ovens, likewise, full of lunch pastries. Cooks were cutting up vegetables, their big knives flashing; others were scaling fish or cutting up beef or preparing chickens or tending the vast stockpots. Behind all this were the massive sinks overflowing with piles of dirty dishes.

"Marcel," said my cicerone to the head chef, a fat man with a face like a thundercloud and angry little black eyes buttressed by big jowls the color of uncooked meat.

I put out my hand, but Marcel Lepage, down on his luck and temporarily embarrassed, was not worthy of such notice—or even of complete sentences. "Get him to the sink. Breaks a dish, see he pays for it. Staff lunch at eleven thirty."

With this I was dismissed. The sous-chef, whose name was Gaston, handed me an apron, and I went to work. While a skinny kitchen boy with bad teeth and a broken nose scraped off the crumbs of bread, rolls, and croissants, the slop of egg yolks, the dried fats of bacons and sausages, the squashed remnants of melons and tomatoes, the thick crusts of oatmeal, I plunged the plates and bowls and cups and saucers into a gray, pond-sized water, parboiling my hands and halfway up to my elbows. Monsieur Lepage was going to earn his passport.

By time for staff lunch, I was wrung out with heat and humidity, as red as the boss, and nearly as shaky as my kitchen boy, whose tendency to let dishes slip had lent excitement to our morning. I was becoming nostalgic for my hitherto despised stint as portrait artiste, when I was seated with the rest and served a respectable stew with a salad, a glass of local red, and a big carafe of water.

Starvation, happily, was not in my future, but amid the noise of the staff table, I found no chance to talk to Gaston, who I sensed would be my best source. Forget the head chef. The Napoleon of the kitchen was as high-strung as a generalissimo before an invasion. He sure had the touch with food, for even the simple staff meal was delicious, but he was terrifying with underlings. Gaston's role, besides actual work with knives and spoons and tricky sauces, was to solve what I guessed were frequent problems with the workforce. He was the one who pulled replacements out of his hat and tempered the storms that overcame the great man at the slightest provocation. If anyone remembered Jerome Chavanel, it would be Gaston.

By late afternoon, our shift was winding down, the Everest of dishes reduced to a humble plateau. I stepped out for a breath of air, my shirt sodden with sweat and dishwater. The lung-catching fumes of Gaulouises Bleu led me to Gaston, who was taking the shade under one of the palm trees.

"How's it going?" he asked.

"I've had worse jobs but none hotter."

"Better in the winter," he said, "though you get acclimated."

"That would take me a while."

"From the north, eh?"

"That's right. And it's funny," I said sensing an opening, "that I wound up here today. One of my distant relatives worked here for quite a while. I'd hoped to meet him on this trip, but I learned recently that he had died."

"Who was that?" Gaston asked.

"His name was Jerome Chavanel. I believe that he was a waiter here."

"You're related to Jerome?" Gaston's expression changed subtly. "Yes, he was in the main dining room—well, it must have been twenty years. Longer than I've been here."

"He must have been good," I said.

"He was good at his job. No one stays at the Negresco, otherwise."

"I had hoped to trace another cousin through him, but I'm out of luck unless you know someone in his family."

"Who's the cousin?"

"A dancer and singer named Cybèle Chavanel. She came south at the end of the war. I thought she might have been in touch with him, since he must have had contacts in the various restaurants and clubs."

"Jerome had contacts everywhere," Gaston said with the faintest hint of disapproval. "And, yes, a young woman did come. That was just before he was killed."

"Killed?"

"Didn't you know? Jerome Chavanel was murdered."

I was uneasy, but Marcel Lepage was horrified. First "Monsieur Renard" shot in London, then "Madame Renard" murdered on the Riviera, followed by the attempt on yours truly, and now this. The old ladies must know how their cousin died and maybe their niece did, too. I wondered if her arrival had precipitated his death.

"Here in Nice?"

"Stabbed as he left work."

After my near miss the other night, I didn't like this at all. "Who did it?"

"The killer was never caught. Well, you can understand, Marcel. Total chaos at the end of the war. Fighting along the Rhine; politicians angling for power. Things got out of hand between the Milice and the Resistance. In all that turmoil," he concluded, "one death more or less—" He gave a particularly expressive shrug.

"I would still like to locate his niece. I have a particular interest in genealogy. I know, I know. Even my family finds that eccentric." Actually, my own family considered me a thorough nuisance and couldn't wait to see the back of me. Monsieur Lepage, I'd decided, had a more conventional rearing.

Gaston did something complicated with his wide thin mouth that managed to express doubt and reluctance and distaste all at once. "Such ladies are floaters," he said. "She started at the Blue Dolphin near the port. She will have moved on, but you might start there. Jerome did claim she had talent."

I thanked him and said that I would. I took counsel with one of the other dishwashers about a room, and by the time the sea faded to black and the lights came on along the Promenade des Anglais, I was dressed up in a dinner jacket and off to find Mademoiselle.

I do like night and going out and drinking and generally carrying on. The ritzy hotels, the ancient port, the mix of fancy money and folk on the make formed a particularly appealing atmosphere, especially when my efforts were all in the interest of duty. That was a novelty, believe me.

After a bit of wandering, I found the Blue Dolphin, a pit with aspirations to becoming a dive. It had a small stage, a greasy bar, watered beer, and an overweight chanteuse in a red gown who gave me the eye. I winked back and he ran his hands through his wig and launched into "The Man I Love" in heavily accented English. The barman, unfortunately, was less susceptible to my charms. He had one of those broad open faces associated with innocence and simplicity, but somewhere along the line both had curdled for him. His expression was blank in repose and sour when engaged. Nice must be very hard up for publicans if he was employed to peddle drinks. He told me that he was relatively new, and he never remembered "the talent."

"This one was young, definitely of the female persuasion, short dark or blond hair. Could dance." I took out the photo the old ladies had given me. "Cybèle Chavanel. I don't know her stage name."

"You don't know much," the barman said.

I bit back a smart answer and launched into my great interest in genealogy, my disappointing visit so far, the brevity of my stay. I also bought him a cognac. It was the latter that inspired him to study both the photo and a little drawing I had made of Cybèle with light hair.

"Oh, yes, Justine," he said after a minute. "Yeah, she could sing. Nice legs, too. Pulled in the Yanks for us for a while."

"Do you know where she went? Or if she is still in the area?"

"She got a gig at one of the fancier clubs. She won't still be there—they shift the headliner every few weeks, but I think she is in the city."

"Justine," I said. "Just the one name?"

"Mademoiselle Justine. That's her stage name."

It wasn't much, but it was more than I'd known earlier. I gave the singer a wave and headed for the glossier clubs around the port and up in the old city. Some had their musical attractions posted, which saved me time but left me thirsty. Others required a drink and a tip for the barman, which was more amusing but emptied my pocket and ate up the evening.

In my pursuit of Mademoiselle Justine, née Cybèle Chavanel, the violet hours turned to midnight and beyond. I was ready to call it a night when I heard music issuing from a café with a few patrons lingering at the sidewalk tables. I went inside and ordered up a Chablis.

On a little stage toward the back, a piano player with an ebony face and spidery fingers worked out some complicated chords, while a bass player plucked away half asleep, his face hidden by the brim of a porkpie hat.

I turned to the barman, gray but still spry at the back end of the evening. "You ever book Mademoiselle Justine?"

"Funny you should ask. You're about"—he turned to check the clock behind the bar—"twenty minutes too late. She just finished her last set."

"Marcel Lepage," I said, sticking out my hand. "We're distant relatives, if this is the right Mademoiselle Justine. I'm down from Rouen. Business trip. I've been trying to track down cousins and such for a genealogical chart. Family thinks I'm crazy, but it's a fun hobby." I was set to go on, as Monsieur Marcel is quite passionate about his avocation, but I could see that the barman was already retreating behind the noncommittal half smile that he doubtless employed on every bore who leaned against his bar. "Any chance I could send her a message or stop by tomorrow and meet her?"

"She starts at ten tomorrow night though she might still be in her dressing room." He leaned down and pressed something under the counter. "I'll just give her a heads-up. Mademoiselle Justine does not like to be caught in dishabille."

I thanked him and tipped him and made my way past the semi-somnolent musicians to the corridor that ran past the toilets. The establishment's offices were dark, but I saw a strip of light underneath the last door. I knocked twice and called, "Mademoiselle Justine?"

"*Entrez.*"

The room was small and cramped with a strong tang of perfume, sweat, and face powder that immediately set me sneezing. "*Pardonnez-moi,*" I said. My eyes were watering, but I could see that the room was empty. Dressing table strewn with cosmetics, street clothes thrown over a chair, a large coatrack holding several gowns with sequins and ruffles. A variety of shoes on the floor. A bunch of flowers in a big glass vase. The only thing missing was Mademoiselle Justine. I only saw her when I looked into the mirror. She had concealed herself behind the door and now she stepped forward. There she was, the woman from the Villa Mimosa, with the same wide face, good features, alert eyes. She was dark now—the blond hair must have been a wig—and she was wearing a scarlet dressing gown instead of the white capris, but what really drew my eye was her new accessory.

I'm no expert on handguns, but this one looked large enough and close enough to do serious damage to both Monsieur Lepage and yours truly.

CHAPTER EIGHT

"Ah, Madame Renard that was," I said and made a little bow.

She started and took a step closer. When she exclaimed, "Oh, it's you!" I guessed that she was seriously nearsighted.

"Marcel Lepage, at your service. Unarmed."

She took the precaution of patting my pockets before motioning for me to sit down on the dressing table stool. "Last time you brought me a package." She leaned against the doorjamb, revolver in hand.

"Last time you were expecting me."

"No, Monsieur, I was expecting someone unknown."

"Now you're expecting someone dangerous."

A moment's hesitation. "At this hour of the night, one can get difficult visitors."

"So I can imagine. But I'm here on a goodwill mission."

She laughed and dropped the revolver into the pocket of her dressing gown. "The aunts sent you."

"That's right. They're worried about you."

She agreed that was possible.

"The deal is this nice new identity and, if I find you, a new passport."

She sniffed. "Is this your usual line of work?"

"Not at all, but I need a passport urgently."

She raised her eyebrows.

"I was seen leaving the Villa Mimosa. Correction, I am the *only* person who was seen leaving the villa. Hence I was first a suspect and then a witness."

"I can't be blamed for the neighbors," she said with a shrug. "They are not responsible for watching the villa."

"Highly selective watching, Mademoiselle. I'm guessing that they were afraid of your associates. And now you are, too."

"Look, Monsieur, I needed money and I did a job. I waited around the villa for four days before you showed up, played the grieving widow, collected the package. That was it."

"And what about Madame Renard? What about her?"

"She never existed," Cybèle said airily. "No more than her husband, I'd guess."

"Yet someone is dead. Someone like you who was pretending to be Madame Renard."

Cybèle crossed her arms. "It was as I told you. Someone was sending a package, I was to be there to collect it. That was all."

"And the name, Mademoiselle? *Renard.* Your aunts felt that came from you. That the name was a message for them."

"Did they?" She looked thoughtful. "Maybe it was, but not from me. I was told the name; I was offered the job. I accepted. I think one's first impulses are always best."

Yours truly agreed, though I sensed that Marcel Lepage had his reservations. "I saw the man called Renard shot in London."

"A scandal and an outrage, I'm sure." She was an odd combination, half genteel bourgeois and half tough artiste.

"No one knows whether he is alive or dead."

"All Europe is a graveyard, Monsieur."

My feelings exactly and a great line for my pals at the Europa, but this was no time to sit around trading profundities. "It is a coincidence impossible to ignore."

"Perhaps he knew the aunts or knew of them. Their papers were always first-rate, real works of art."

"Attracting clients both desirable and undesirable?"

"I wouldn't know," she said. "The aunts did not share that side of the business with me. I had other functions."

I would have liked to learn some more about those, but her face darkened, closing off that line of inquiry. "Your aunts are prudent; maybe you are not. You seemed nervous at the villa. I thought that you were tempted to delay my departure."

"Dream on," she said. "Though it was certainly boring in the villa. I'd been told a day, an evening at the most."

"You were relieved after the package had been examined."

"I was relieved my job was done. It was a favor. For a friend of a friend. One of those things."

"And now you keep a gun in your dressing room. The aunts will not be pleased to learn about that."

"The aunts are fanciful and not to be trusted. That's free advice you would be wise to take."

"People can be dishonest and still care about you."

"You can tell them that I am alive and well and earning my living on the boards. How's that for your report?"

"I think they would like you to give them that report in person. If you feel able to return, that is."

"What do you mean, 'able to return'?"

"They told me about your—misfortune at the end of the war."

"Really." She narrowed her eyes in a way that reminded me strongly of Agathe Chavanel. If nothing else, I believed that she was their niece. "What did they tell you?"

"About the young German soldier, his loss, the revenge of your neighbors."

She laughed then, a hoarse, bitter laugh that seemed years older than her fresh face.

"Your short hair suggested—"

"A mere theatrical convenience. Mademoiselle Justine is a woman of infinite variety." She came over to the dressing table and fiddled with her coiffeur. "The aunts are incredible."

"None of this was true?"

"None of it is true and all of it. A paradox, Monsieur, that I do not intend to explore with you. Get on the morning train, tell the aunts, and collect your pay." She gave me a serious look. "You would be wise to do that."

Just then a small bulb flashed once, twice, dyeing our faces red. At this signal from the barman Cybèle froze.

"A visitor?" I stood up but she shook her head.

"The back exit is locked."

I grabbed a scarf, wrapped it around my hand, and loosened two of the four bare lightbulbs burning over her dressing table. The room, which had been deeply shadowed beyond their glare now sank into a brown twilight pierced by the two solitary lights. She pulled me over to the large coatrack and pushed me behind her evening gowns. I draped one over my head, pulled my arms into my sides, and hid behind the rest. Whoops. Feet showing. I stepped up on the base of the rack and let one dress down to the ground. I was precariously balanced, trapped in satin and surrounded by sequins, when someone knocked on the door.

"*Entrez.*" Her voice was steady. The aunts, I thought, would be pleased.

"You alone?" A low masculine voice edged with menace. Normally just my dish but under the present circumstances more excitement than I needed.

"Of course."

"Jean said you had a visitor."

"He left. Jean must have been in the cellar. The usual." She gave a little barking laugh. "I have my admirers, but so many are peculiar."

"This place is dark as a tomb. How do you see to put on your makeup?"

"Long practice. What do you want, Richard?"

"To see you, of course."

"You could have come to my show, *chérie*. I was rather good tonight." She hummed a tune and, through a fringe of feathers, I saw her pivot into a dance turn dangerously near my flimsy barricade. I hoped she wouldn't get carried away.

Her visitor made no reply. He lingered by the door, a heavy presence like a storm front. I could just see his silhouette reflected in the mirror, and I realized that, with a step or two to the left, he would undoubtedly spot me in the glass.

"I need a better venue," Cybèle continued. "Look at this dressing room." Perhaps she had spotted the danger of the mirror, too, for she perched on the dressing table, careless of her cosmetics and paints. She crossed her legs cool as could be and unwrapped a chocolate. I began to see how the Chavanels had survived the war. "You did say you had contacts at good clubs."

"Sure, sure," he said impatiently. "If all goes well, we can buy a club, never mind get you booked into one. Serge told you that."

"You got what you wanted, didn't you? I thought everything was set."

"There have been some complications."

"Not my worry," she said. "And I'm not sure I want to know about them." Out of the corner of my eye, I saw her tilt her head. She had a nice line of movie star gestures, and I had the unsettling feeling that every move she made was for effect, that the whole personality of Mademoiselle Justine, chanteuse and danseuse, was a conscious construction.

"Serge says the cop has let us down. He had a suspect, he had witnesses. Now the suspect's done a bunk, and he says the evidence isn't good enough, anyway. No magistrate would accept it."

I was so angry that I almost gave myself away. I should be off, passport in hand, with the inspector waving bon voyage. Instead I was torturing my sinuses with stale perfume and hiding in drag like an extra in a French farce.

"Whose fault is that?" she asked.

"Look, you let people cross you in this business and pretty soon you have no business left."

"Like the theatrical business. You let people use you, and they don't know when to stop."

"It's not like that, baby," he said. His voice practically creaked with exertion, as if romantic charm wasn't natural to him. He leaned toward her, and in the harsh light of the dressing table I caught a strongly featured face, a deep tan, short black hair. He was older than she was, and I guessed more my type than hers. "You've got to talk to the old ladies. They're in this somehow, the cop says."

"I will not involve them."

He grabbed the front of her dressing gown. "It's not up to you. You do what you're told or there's space in the fish locker. Understand?"

I took a deep breath. With one word, even a gesture, she could clear the aunts and rid herself of me.

Instead, she said, "Get yourself another 'Madame Renard.'"

He reached down and there was the dull glint of something in his hand. I stepped off the rack and gave it a shove. He had barely registered my appearance in red-and-black satin when a thunderous explosion pounded into my ears, the tiny dressing room shuddered, and Cybèle's visitor listed toward the dressing table. The knife rattled onto the floor followed by a dark wash of blood, while the smell of gunpowder and various bodily wastes expanded in the air. Still, he seemed suspended, falling in slow motion. Then his head crashed the corner of the dressing table; his hand cleared a collection of powders, paints, lipsticks, perfumes; a rain of little bottles and pots bounced onto the floor. Cybèle stood frozen with the gun in her hand. No surprise: Violent death is an all-encompassing experience.

When I said, "Best put that down," she swung the weapon toward me. "Marcel Lepage," I reminded her, as I disentangled myself from a feather boa and a long black number with beading, "dispatched from the aunts, at your service."

She came back to herself after a few seconds, took a deep breath, and looked at the revolver, which she laid on the dressing table. "Is he dead, do you think?"

I tightened up the bulbs to give us more light and stepped back into the Blitz with its bomb victims and blackout accidents. I checked for a pulse in the carotid artery and in the wrist, checked the heartbeat, checked for any signs of breath. Strictly routine in this case, because she had shot him from a foot away with a heavy military revolver, another little souvenir of a rotten time. I stood up and nodded my head.

"I'm not sorry," she said, though her voice wavered. "He murdered that woman for nothing and kept her body in the fish locker. I don't know why that makes it worse, but it does."

I had to agree. "Who was he?"

"Richard Malet. He worked in the black market then for Serge Brun, who went from the Resistance to running dodgy clubs." She folded her arms across her body and began to sway back and forth.

"You need a drink," I said. "Have you anything?"

She shook her head. Figuring that if the shot hadn't brought the barman, he must be long gone, I went through to the club and liberated a bottle of brandy and two glasses. When she had drunk enough to stop shivering, I said, "What now? It was self-defense, you have a witness. We have the knife. I think we call the gendarmes."

She shook her head violently. "He has associates, including at least one *flic*."

"Inspector Chardin."

"So I believe."

"You have somewhere to go? We pretend this all happened after you left?"

"Nowhere far enough." She took a breath. "I think he must disappear, and I'll need your help. One way or the other." She picked up the revolver again.

Another little moment of decision for yours truly. I didn't think she'd shoot—though doubtless the late Richard Malet had labored under the same impression—but I didn't much fancy meeting the gendarmes either.

"Count me in," I said. "What do you want me to do?"

"We need to get him out of here. Clean up the floor, lose the knife."

"The knife stays with him. If he's found, it's your defense."

She thought for a minute and agreed to this. I was sent to fetch the key to the rear door and the curtain from the small stage in the club, while she changed into a pair of slacks and a sweater and fetched a bucket and water to clean the floor. That was patently hopeless—the floor had been filthy even before Richard's sudden demise. We mopped up the worst of the blood, wrapped Richard in the curtain, and hauled him to the back exit.

The rear door led to a combined alley and parking space. There were trash cans, a broken umbrella, empty wine crates, and a small van with the name of the club emblazoned on its sides. We stood looking at the vehicle for a minute. The ultimate result of circumventing the UK postal service was the projected disposal of a body with La Fille Dorée's van. Fortunately, my researches in the clubs and cafés had left me in a semianesthetized state, and a good jolt of brandy had somewhat detached Cybèle from the bizarre here and now. "Can you drive?" she asked.

"Sorry, no. I'm strictly Tube and taxis in London."

"The aunts might have sprung for someone professional," she said sourly.

"Someone professional would have ended this caper an hour ago." That shut her up. Cybèle opened the back of the van, and we lifted Richard, trussed in red velvet like a dead cardinal and stinking like an abattoir, into the back. She returned to the club, locked the rear door from the inside, and emerged at the front door wearing, I was thankful to see, a pair of spectacles. Though they gave her an air of intellect and competence, I asked if she could drive.

"Theoretically," she said. She put her large shoulder bag behind the seat and started the motor. Her difficulties with the clutch and the gears revealed the gap between theory and practice. The little van hopped like a bunny, snarled, creaked, and backfired like a whole menagerie. On the third try, she hit the right combination, and we rolled out of the alley and onto the deserted streets.

"Next stop the fish locker?"

"Poetic justice, but no. He would be found too soon by the wrong people, and they might guess who'd put him there."

"The water?" I asked hopefully, because I could not imagine that the van's halting progress was going to get us very far.

"The tide would bring him back in. He needs to disappear," she added, "as if he had never been."

"Like Victor Renard?"

"Very like," she said. "We have to get up into the hills."

"And back before the club workers return."

"Exactly." She ground the gears again.

After a circuitous route through the streets of the old quarter, we reached the road north to Saint-André-de-la-Roche, Falicon, and Les Moulins. Once away from cross-streets and traffic lights, Cybèle did better, though as the road grew steeper, downshifting became an adventure. However, she knew where she wanted to go, turning with difficulty but without hesitation onto narrower and steeper roads as we climbed farther and farther from the coast.

We went so far that I asked. "Do we have enough gas?"

She looked down at the gauge. "There should be a can in the back," she said in a way that did not reassure me. The only thing worse than driving to the back of beyond with Richard would be getting stranded with him in the desolate hills.

All at once, Cybèle hit the brakes, stalling the van. "Missed our turn," she said and began the serious business of reversing. Apparently reverse is a tricky gear, for we jerked forward and stalled several times, before the stars aligned for us and we shot backward toward a track that only she could see. "*Voilà!*" she shouted.

The waning moonlight revealed a faint indentation running between the brush and grasses. Two tries later, she steered the van into the opening, and we went bouncing along what it would have been a courtesy to call a goat track.

"Wouldn't anywhere do here?" I asked.

"We have to be able to turn around," she said, "and we don't have a shovel."

Too true. At last, after a gauntlet of overgrown brush, rocks, and ruts, we approached a low, stone building with a small cleared area in front. Cybèle managed to turn the van so its nose pointed in the general direction of the track, the road, and civilization. She hopped out and opened the back. Richard had come partly unrolled, which was disagreeable, and we found the gas can was only half full, which might be serious.

We laid Richard out on the ground, and while I filled the van's tank, Cybèle went to a sort of lean-to attached to one end of the building. She lit a match and checked the door before summoning me for help. While I lit one match after another, she fiddled with the latch until the door swung loose. Inside, we found an old rake, some miscellaneous machine parts, and, toward the back in a cobwebbed alcove, a pickax. I carried this outside to where we'd left Richard. "Anywhere in particular?" I asked.

She hesitated for the first time and stood for a moment considering our options. "The back, I think. There's an old goat pen."

Great. It's amazing how often life throws me an agricultural googly. I escaped horses and dogs and cows and country life with my lungs semi-intact at sixteen, yet no escape is permanent. I followed her behind the building into what had once been a stone-walled pen and was now drifting back into scrub. "Easier digging but harder to conceal," I said.

"Perhaps under the stones," she said.

There was that. I moved a couple of the stones that had tumbled from the wall and tested the earth beneath with the pickax. Have I mentioned that manual labor is another thing I detest? This was dusty work, and after we carried Richard around and I started coughing and wheezing, Cybèle had to take a turn with the pickax.

"You won't die, will you?" She was a cool customer, but the idea of two corpses in one night was more than she wanted to handle.

"Dust," I gasped. "Old agricultural dust is the absolute worst."

I watched her labor for a while, and then we organized to divide the work. I swung the pickax, and she pulled the earth away with her hands. The dry ground was hard, and Richard seemed unconscionably tall, but at last we had excavated one of the shallow graves that so often show up in Nan's favored crime stories. I now understood why, but given that the sky was lightening in the east we could do no better. We dragged Richard to what I hoped would be his final resting place, and we were ready to lay him in, when I thought about his pockets. "Better if he has no papers on him," I said.

Cybèle straightened up and nodded. She unwrapped the curtain, but said, "I don't want to touch him."

Although I didn't much like the idea myself, I gingerly patted his shirt and slid my hand quickly in and out of his pants pockets. I came up with a wallet and a set of keys.

There was no time for examination. We tipped him in, and Cybèle pushed and kicked the dirt over him, lamenting her chipped nails and damaged shoes, before, with what I feared might be my last few good breaths, I wrestled the fallen stones over the raw dirt.

"It looks like a grave with a few stones over it," she said, which I thought was true but unhelpful. She scrambled over the remains of wall and started banging at the stones with the pickax. I joined her and, by leaning with all our weight on the loosened stones, we precipitated a small landslide. With this, she was satisfied. We returned the pickax, brushed off our clothes and hands the best we could, and got back in the van. As she was warming up the van's engine, Cybèle looked at me. "Tell the aunts you deserve that passport," she said.

CHAPTER NINE

The night's drinks had long since metabolized and even La Fille Dorée's brandy had worn off by the time we approached the city. I regretted having left the bottle behind. I think that gravediggers must be heavy drinkers, because it's a serious thing to put anyone into the ground, even a stranger, even someone like the late, un-lamented Richard Malet. I think Cybèle felt that, too, because she seemed subdued and didn't swear at the gears when she had dif-ficulties shifting anymore. Perhaps that was the moment when I should have broached her return to the old ladies, but I was preoc-cupied with my own difficulties. I could see nothing to be gained and much to lose in staying beyond the first morning train. The sooner I forgot this night's work, the better.

A few delivery vans and work trucks had appeared on the streets, and the tardy southern light brightened the sea as we approached La Fille Dorée. Cybèle had begun elaborate preparations with the brake, the clutch, and the gearshift, when I saw a black truck at the side of the building.

"Someone's parked in back."

She slammed on the brakes, stalled the van, of course, struggled with reverse, of course, and stalled again before we shot out into the street, which was, fortunately, empty. We took off at high speed, the gears grinding and protesting. Cybèle had turned quite white—and I don't think it was just from her difficulties with the motor. Careless of our depleted fuel, she seemed set to run us right out of town.

"That was the truck from the fish locker," she said. "It will be full of ice for deliveries."

Ah. "La Fille Dorée doesn't serve fish, does it?"

"No. They were probably coming for me."

That was my thought as well. Lucky for us, Malet had been taken by surprise, or both of us might have wound up in the cooler with the sole and mackerel. Not a good thought.

Cybèle pulled into a narrow street with modest apartment buildings, small hotels, and pensions and stopped. "Serge has a flat here, but we'll have to be quick." She locked the van and we hustled up the outside stairs of a two-story white stone construction. At the top, two windows and a peeling wooden door opened onto a narrow terrace. The door, unsurprisingly, was locked.

"You haven't a key."

"I thought you might find a way to get in."

At that point, I had to agree that the aunts should have hired a professional. Both windows were closed with metal shutters. I stepped back and noticed an open roof window set into the slates. "Are you good with heights? I can lift you easier than you can lift me."

Cybèle kicked off her shoes and laid down her bag. She put one strong dancer's foot on my bent knee and gripped the edge of the roof. I grabbed her waist and pushed. She got a grip on the tiles, slithered back. I hoisted her left knee, then she was up and crawling toward the window. A creak of metal as she hauled it all the way open, then her long white-clad legs, striped shirt, and dark head disappeared through the opening and down into the room below. Thump. In the ensuing silence, I took the opportunity to open her bag and slip the revolver into my waistband. A moment later, the door opened. Cybèle looked dirty and scuffed, but this time there were no complaints. "Quick," she said. "We don't have any time to spare."

"Right," I said and handed her the bag. "Just what are we doing?"

"We're finding the package, of course."

"You think he still has it?"

"I suspect he couldn't make head nor tail of it. Which isn't surprising for Serge. You take the front room. I'll take the bedroom."

I waded in, literally. Serge's living room had a couch, an upholstered chair, a table, and two wooden chairs. There was theoretically a rug on the floor—I caught a glimpse of brown and maroon flowers—but it was covered with fading newspapers, some magazines, clothes, a blanket, and wine bottles, all empty, alas, plus a pair of old boots and a blue smock like the ones the men at the villa had worn. A shotgun of some type leaned in one corner, and there were a number of smallish wooden crates, all nailed shut. I hoped he hadn't hidden the package in one of those. The whole place was saturated with cigarette smoke, which served to take the edge off the sweat and spilled wine aroma that lingered around the clothes.

I was sifting the floor debris, when Cybèle called from the bedroom, "Marcel!"

She was holding the notebook. "This is it, yes?"

I looked over her shoulder as she flipped through the pages. I recognized the columns of names and numbers. "Wasn't there a letter, too?"

"You lied to me. You said you hadn't opened it."

Time for my version of the Gallic shrug. "I couldn't say I learned anything from it. Or from the letter."

The sound of a heavy motor outside cut off discussion. Cybèle ran to the front windows and peeked through the shutters. *"Merde."*

Two men were standing by the car; both were large and one, balding. "Golden dome was at the Villa Mimosa," I said, and Cybèle said, "Serge is the other one. We'll get out through the roof. They won't look up."

I hoped that she was right. In the bathroom, which was as insalubrious as the rest of the flat, she stepped onto the sink and grabbed the sill of the roof window. With a little help from me, she wiggled onto the roof.

"Quick, Marcel."

I got onto the sink, the metal supports and pipes creaking. I was taller than Cybèle, so I got a good grip on the sill, but being both larger and less flexible, I was only halfway out when I heard voices on the terrace. Cybèle flattened herself against the tiles, a foot away from where I was dangling. Most of my weight was on my midsection, and I sincerely hoped the safety on her revolver was operational. Cybèle raised her head a fraction, shook it, and gave me a panicked look.

Below us, Serge was fiddling with his keys—perhaps he was a bit the worse for wear; perhaps, like grave digging, stashing bodies in the fish locker requires lubrication. As the door creaked open, I got my hips through the window and out onto the tiles. Below I heard them shouting for Richard, and with this as inspiration, I scraped my legs out the window. Cybèle pushed it shut before we slithered to the edge of the roof, dropped onto the terrace, and ran down the stairs.

"Leave it," Cybèle said, when I put my hand on the van door. "They'll think Richard drove it here."

We left the street for a series of alleys running behind hotels with their trash cans and discarded bed frames, and small shops that smelled of fish, sawdust, and old vegetables. We emerged several streets away from Serge's apartment, and I flagged down the first taxi I spotted.

"To the station." I said. When Cybèle couldn't come up with a better idea, she followed me into the cab.

We caught the morning train west, found seats in an empty compartment, and assessed our options. Mine were not flourishing. I was carrying a murder weapon of uncertain provenance, and I had no international papers and very little cash. At this point, I remembered Malet's wallet. The brown leather billfold revealed a gratifying amount of money and some little scraps of paper with names and phone numbers. I transferred the money and papers to my wallet, threw the billfold out the window, and settled down to study the cool, whitish light on the Mediterranean.

After a time, Cybèle said, "The aunts will be our best bet."

"Though someone may still be watching the *gare*."

"We will get off before. The train has to slow just before it reaches town. We used to jump off as kids to save the walk home."

"And then what?"

"You said that they owed you a passport. You get it and leave."

"Leaving you with the notebook?"

"It's mine, now," she said.

"I am under pressure from a gambler named Joubert to retrieve the notebook—and that missing letter. Friends of mine have been threatened."

"You will have to negotiate with the aunts," she said. "They may even know this Joubert. We had refugees from everywhere, all desperate, most unscrupulous, some clever."

"And in need of the aunts' skill?"

"Yes," she said soberly. "The aunts were very much in demand."

"And you?" I asked. "You would have been what? Fifteen? Sixteen?"

"Thereabouts." She got up, lowered the window, and stared at the black rocks, the flat, pale water, and the hamlets with their white walled houses topped by dusty red and gray tiles. She didn't move until the train pulled away from the village below the Villa Mimosa, and we made our way along the swaying corridor. We jumped as the train slowed for the level crossing at a jumble of houses, small businesses, and overgrown lots and gardens. A few hundred yards along, Cybèle turned up a narrow side street, and I realized that we were near Pierre's bicycle shop. In a town this size, he had to have known her.

Cybèle took an unfamiliar and circuitous route to the aunts' back garden. She reached up one of the pillars flanking the gate, took down a key, and let us into the shadows beneath the cypresses. The house shutters were open for the morning sun, and as we reached the terrace, Aunt Anastasie stepped out one of the French doors.

"Monsieur Lepage," she said. "You have exceeded all our expectations."

I entered the house in the unaccustomed role of the returned hero, to be feted with some of Agathe's fine pastries and good coffee. Nothing was said about the notebook, the letter, or the reasons for our hasty arrival, dusty and disheveled, and carrying nothing except Cybèle's shoulder bag. Instead, we sat companionably in the parlor, gorging on little cakes and tarts and slices of an early melon. It struck me that the ladies were being excessively polite and discreet about our situation, and I was about to open negotiations for Cybèle's revolver and the meaning of the notebook, when I felt unaccountably sleepy.

True, I had been up all night, but I am used to seeing the midnight hour and all the little hours that follow it without missing the morning light in the studio. I set down my coffee cup on a table that seemed an unaccountably long way away. My hand felt strange, too, as if it had swollen up and floated away from my arm, which was, in turn, growing heavy as were my eyelids. I leaned my head against the plush sofa and tried without success to keep the chandelier from rotating, then darkness overcame the plaster decorations on the ceiling and dropped down the walls and furniture to sweep me away.

I woke up in a high, old-fashioned bed that reminded me of Berlin and my wicked uncle Lastings and various adventures of a misspent youth. The light had faded in the garden and the house was very quiet. I guessed late afternoon. The nice old ladies had drugged me and, I saw, made off with my dinner jacket, slacks, and shirt. All were admittedly very dirty, but that meant the revolver—and maybe Malet's cash—were gone. In recompense, I saw a clean set of clothes awaiting me.

I was sitting on the bed, buttoning the shirt, when Aunt Anastasie tapped on the door. "Ah, *cher Monsieur Francis*, you are awake."

"Don't *cher Monsieur* me; you slipped me a Mickey Finn. If we were in Shanghai, I'd be enslaved on some filthy freighter by now."

"My apologies," she said, and I must say, "*désolée*" made regrets sound better in French. "But please understand," she said, sitting down in the chair. "We did not want to take any risks, because we have waited a very long time for this material. Not this, of course," she added and handed me back my wallet stuffed with Malet's bills. "We are not thieves."

"Well, I am. These"—I ruffled the bills—"belonged to a dubious type named Richard Malet."

"Yes, so we have heard. And we are grateful for your assistance, but you had taken Cybèle's revolver, and we were not sure what game you were playing."

I was indignant. "The game I was playing was trying to locate your niece. I arrived just before she shot Malet. Admittedly, after provocation. He worked for Serge Brun who apparently stores corpses in a fish locker."

"You know, we made Serge his first set of false papers." Her voice almost sounded nostalgic. "One did not ask too many questions then. Life was terrible and full of complications and yet we had no doubts."

"And now?"

"Now there is nothing but doubts. With your help, we can put some to rest."

"Where's my passport?" I asked. "I did your paintings, I found your niece. I want to go back to London."

"We very much need your help."

I shook my head. "I very much need to get back to London, preferably with that notebook. I have been threatened. Nan, too."

"Nan? Who is Nan?"

"My old nanny and companion. She is going blind and cannot be left alone too much longer."

"I see. You continue to surprise me, Monsieur Francis. But in a good way." She smiled and tapped my knee in a friendly gesture.

"Another difficulty is that Monsieur Joubert, who holds my gambling chits, expects me to retrieve the notebook."

"That might be arranged, but we must discuss this all together," she said, standing up. "We will fix you something to eat and we will talk."

They were waiting in the parlor when I came downstairs, and I had a moment to wonder how they had managed to transport me to the bedroom above. Cybèle and Aunt Agathe sat together on the sofa, while Anastasie had taken a straight-backed chair before the window. There was a plate with *pâté en croûte*, some small tomatoes, and bottles of mineral water set out on the low table. I found I was hungry. When I had finished two slices of the *pâté*, Anastasie said, "You must tell us about this Monsieur Joubert."

"I delivered the package for him." I explained that he had opened a London gambling club just as the war was ending and described his curious behavior the night that Victor Renard was shot. The old ladies listened with complete concentration. They wanted to know every detail of the shooting and exactly what Victor Renard looked like. By the time I'd explained Joubert's visit to the studio and his proposal, they exchanged glances and nodded.

"I think we know this man," said Agathe.

"It is László Bencze, to the life," Anastasie agreed. "He was a resident alien during the war. He had money, and, unlike so many, he managed to hold on to his capital and become an associate of Paul Desmarais."

"We think, in fact," Agathe said, "that he funded some of Paul's activities. Early on, that is. Later, Paul needed no help."

"And Renard. Is he Desmarais?"

The sisters looked at each other and thought this over. "Maybe," said Agathe. "But the relationship does not sound right. Paul was a very commanding, dominating figure. László was sly and cautious. He was careful always to defer to Paul."

I pointed out that Renard had been bleeding to death.

"And may be dead," Anastasie said. "Was that not Monsieur Joubert's information?"

"It was and his possession of the package suggests that it is true. But if so, the information did not reach the public press."

"We must find out," Anastasie said. "We will do that."

I guessed that they would somehow enlist Inspector Chardin

for this task. "But what is in the notebook?" I asked. "What is so valuable about it?"

"In itself not very much. It is a record of Desmarais's dealings with various people. People you do not know, Monsieur Francis, but people who are now important in the Var and who wish to leave the war behind. That is one thing."

"The other names," Agathe added, "represent outright thefts."

"*Almost* outright," her sister corrected. "Paul was one of our contacts early on. He introduced people who needed papers. Which we supplied."

"While he took most of their valuables as his commission?" I guessed.

"Exactly. We did not know this at first, and once we realized, we were compromised. You can imagine our position."

I could, actually. "And what do you plan to do with the notebook?"

"It will be evidence in a trial that is to begin soon. Important evidence." She held up her hand. "But it is not impossible to return it to Monsieur Joubert. Not at all."

I must have looked puzzled for she added, "the magic of photography."

"We developed a certain expertise doing passport photos," Agathe said.

"I don't understand why Joubert wanted to send the documents to France in the first place," I said. "Surely, he might also be implicated."

Cybèle spoke up. "There's a little more to it."

Her aunts looked displeased, but she said, "He probably saved my life. He certainly helped me out of a tough spot. And he knows Joubert."

"Paul ended up a very wealthy man. We believe—" Anastasie began.

"We know," interrupted her sister.

"All right, we know that he hid his money in Swiss banks. We think that the letter and the notebook together might form a cipher."

"And now?"

"Well, in any case, we do not have the letter, but we think that there may be a third piece."

"Why is that?"

"Because otherwise nothing else would have been needed. There would have been no reason to involve this 'Madame Renard,' far less murder the poor woman. I think there was some other document that was the key for the rest."

"Belonging to the late 'Madame Renard'?"

"Possibly."

"It is our best guess. Which Serge was too stupid to perceive. His thought was to murder her and have Cybèle take her place. Once he had the package, he didn't know what to do with it."

The thugs of my acquaintance in London were not always very bright either, but the whole affair was peculiar. "Why wouldn't Joubert put the package in the mail if he wanted it sent? Why didn't he trust the post?"

Anastasie frowned. "Perhaps the post was watched. Perhaps one of the postal workers was corrupt."

Agathe shook her head. "I think that he wanted her dead. And, Monsieur Francis, he planned for you to be blamed."

Anastasie agreed. "When you delayed the delivery, Serge grew impatient. Or Madame Renard stopped cooperating."

"But who was she?"

"That's what we'd like you to find out."

"Oh, no. I found Cybèle, whom you could have found quite nicely on your own. Give me the notebook, and I'll see that Joubert gets it back."

They shook their heads. "Have him come here," Anastasie said. "Tell him you know where it is; tell him you can arrange an exchange."

"A mutually beneficial exchange," Agathe added. Her smile gave me pause.

"In the meantime," Anastasie began, "you might undertake a little exploration."

I refused absolutely, although I did agree to contact Joubert, or rather, to wire Arnold and have him open negotiations with Joubert, who was to appear in person in three days' time to retrieve his package.

CHAPTER TEN

The household went into high gear immediately. The aunts retired to their darkroom. Hidden under a big hat and one of the aunts' long skirts, Cybèle was dispatched for a series of phone calls at the nearest public booth, and yours truly was left to mourn the loss of various cafés and bistros. I sat in the garden, studied the cypresses, and thought about Van Gogh, whose brush turned them to pillars of black fire.

Early the next morning, we received the return wire: Joubert would come at the end of the week. He gave us his arrival time and expected me to meet him at the station. In the meantime, the aunts urged the utmost caution, as to venture out casually might endanger everyone. After my experiences in the nighttime town, I was inclined to agree, though I find caution disagreeable and abstinence untenable. Indeed, it was strictly boredom that led me to so complicate my life.

Anastasie had taken a break from whatever she and Agathe were doing with the notebook and my passport to be. When she saw me sulking on the terrace, she came out and asked if I would like to see the finished dollhouse. I followed her into the front room where the sawdust smell had vanished and the paint had dried to the faintest odor of turpentine and oil.

The house was complete. The ancestor portrait hung over the mantel in its gold frame, and the "fresco" was mounted on the ceiling. Diminutive tubs of flowers and two small conifers flanked the front steps, and miniature sling chairs sat on the back terrace. "It is delightful, Madame," I said honestly. "Charming."

"Your contribution was invaluable," she said.

"And you've added figures." To be honest, I had looked first for my workmanship and had only just noticed that a family of sorts had been added. There was a man, nicely dressed to the nines, lying in the front foyer. "He's tumbled over," I said and reached to pick him up.

"No, no, Monsieur Francis. He is quite dead. And see here." She pointed to a blonde woman, also dressed in evening clothes, standing on the stair landing. On closer inspection, I saw a tiny revolver.

"Very dramatic. Do you stage murders in all your houses?"

"This was a special order. Rather a provocation, I suspect."

"Does it represent a real house?"

She nodded.

"And the murder?"

"That, too. No one you would know," she added, which made me think the house was somehow germane to our present situation, but she said no more. "It's to be delivered today. Would you like to go along? The house really needs two or three people to lift it safely."

"How are you getting it there?"

"One of Cybèle's old friends rents a van for us on these occasions. Pierre is such a nice boy. He runs the bicycle repair shop. Perhaps you've seen it."

My prospects brightened instantly. "I could give him a hand," I said.

He arrived within the hour in a dark green paneled van. Anastasie introduced me as Marcel Lepage, and Pierre, obviously a man of parts, accepted this with a straight face and shook my hand. I gave him a wink when Anastasie was not looking. We opened the front gate, sacrificing a few flowers and a strip of lawn to pull the van up to the front of the house, then muscled the dollhouse, swaddled in moving quilts and supported on its heavy plywood base, out to the van. It barely fit, and we both had scraped knuckles before our cargo was safely stowed. Anastasie gave Pierre a set of rapid-fire directions and cautions, then we headed east. Once under way, I promised Pierre a fine lunch.

"Were you questioned again by the police?" he asked.

I do love a man with a sense of humor. "No, I've branched out. And you've obviously remembered Cybèle."

"Old habits," he said by way of explanation. "During the war, nobody knew anybody. It gets to be a habit."

"I suspect the old ladies have kept quite a few wartime habits."

He shrugged.

Wrong ploy. "They wanted me to find Cybèle and now they want me to find where the late Madame Renard hid something valuable."

"They want to find where she lived, you mean?"

"Maybe. But maybe she left—whatever—at the Villa Mimosa."

He thought this over. "We might check. On the way back."

"You know who has the keys?"

"It is to be rented. Of course, the tenant would have to be someone foreign who does not know its history."

I liked the idea, but I was not sure that I looked prosperous enough.

"Everyone knows the English are eccentric," he said. "And an English painter—"

I agreed we would give it a try. For the rest of the trip, we discussed the bike race. In between details of the mountain stages and time trials, I snuck in a few questions about the buyer of the dollhouse, but all I got from Pierre was that the man was rich and eccentric, which made him sound like a good candidate for the Villa Mimosa.

Finally, I asked, "Did you know about the dolls?"

I saw his surprise.

"No, you couldn't have, as the house was already wrapped up. They've staged a murder."

Pierre took his eyes off the road and met mine. "A murder?"

"Yes, a little man in evening dress—beautifully done, I might add—and a woman in a red gown. He's lying in the foyer and she's halfway down the main staircase holding a revolver."

"Really!" said Pierre. His expression was unreadable.

"What's the matter?"

"Just a coincidence. During the war a local man was murdered in his front hall. I remember people talking about it." He gave me his beautiful smile before turning all his attention to the road winding through a neighborhood of fine villas with lush gardens and sea views. He slowed the van at a white gravel drive lined with palms, oleanders, and cypresses. At the end was a large pink villa with fine stone trim and a graveled parking area. Pierre went round to the tradesman's entrance, while I opened the back of the van.

A moment later, a pale, self-important domestic with black patent hair and shadowed eyes emerged. I guessed he was the butler, for despite the heat, he'd topped his shirt and tie and dark pants with a long striped apron as if he'd been hard at work cleaning old family silver or dusting off the wine cellar. He inspected the cargo, still shrouded in its packing, then directed us up the front steps and into the main foyer, where the miniature villa was to reside on top of a large and beautifully carved bureau.

Pierre cut the strings holding the packing blankets in place, and we gradually unwrapped the Chavanels' handiwork. I heard him take in his breath as the façade of the little building was revealed. I raised my eyebrows.

"Amazing detail," he said.

We had just lifted it into place when a door opened farther down the hall. The old man limping toward us had long white hair and thick white eyebrows above sharp black eyes. His high forehead was white, his cheeks eroded, his chin wobbly, and his head thrust forward by the curvature of his spine. The hands gripping his stout black cane seemed too big for the remnants age had left of his body, but he was dressed with care in an ancient summer suit, and all his accessories were elegant except for a pair of ugly black orthopedic shoes. Although Pierre greeted him and I nodded, he did not acknowledge us in any way until he had studied the house for several minutes, and I had opened the side panels for him. He paid particular attention to the figures and made a slight adjustment to the dead man who had shifted in transit from his pool of blood.

"*Merveilleuse.* The ladies have not lost their skill. You may tell them that I am perfectly satisfied."

I assured him that his compliments would be conveyed.

"Are you, Monsieur, perhaps the painter they mentioned?"

"I assisted on the petite fresco and the portrait."

He took out a magnifying glass and peered at both. "A reasonable approximation," was his verdict. "You are to be congratulated, as well. And you"—he turned to Pierre—"what do you think?"

Pierre hesitated a moment. "It will be a unique decoration, Monsieur."

"It will be an accusation," he said and through sheer force of will straightened out of his habitual half crouch. "That bitch fooled the police. She cowed my younger relatives with threats of libel and slander. But not me. Everyone who comes will understand my opinion without my saying a word. I will ruin her." He gave a short, barking laugh.

He struck me as ingenious and unpleasant in roughly equal amounts. I allowed that it was an elegant solution.

"Do you agree?" he asked, turning to Pierre, who shrugged. I thought that my friend looked uncomfortable.

"I don't know you, do I?" the old man asked.

"I think not, Monsieur. Unless you've ever had need of a bicycle."

"You are some sort of mechanic?"

"I run the bicycle shop in town. It was my father's."

The old man's expression changed instantly. "Mechanics are the bane of this earth," he cried furiously. "Get out of my house!" He raised his cane, and I think he would have struck Pierre, if my friend had not sidestepped nimbly and backed down the hall. The old man limped after him, screaming and cursing so loudly that he attracted the butler, who came running in a state of high anxiety. "What is wrong, sir?"

"He just discovered that Pierre is a bike mechanic."

"Monsieur Lambert cannot endure mechanics," the butler said.

"He must think vans drive themselves."

"Monsieur Lambert has nothing to do with vans," the butler exclaimed as if I had suggested bottom pinching on the *plage*, which might, indeed, have been his game. "He'll be in such a state!"

He ran to the door where his boss was clinging to the door casement and preparing to descend the steps. "Come, come, sir, you must not upset yourself." The butler took his arm. "Let us help you inside. The noonday heat is very bad, the doctor says." He looked over his shoulder at me and said, "Come help me with him."

I couldn't say I was keen, given his blanket condemnation of a useful part of the populace, but I gestured for Pierre to move the van away. Then the butler took one arm, I took the other, and we more or less dragged the old fellow down the hall to a large, dark bedroom. He was swearing and muttering at every step, but I had the feeling that he was not as upset as his faithful butler seemed to think, and indeed, when offered a sedative, the old rascal called loudly for a cognac.

I settled him in a chair and the butler returned with a bottle and a snifter glass on a tray.

"Thank you. He will be all right now," said the butler when we were back in the front hall. As if sensing some explanation was required, he added, "Monsieur Lambert has bad, bad memories. Though he commissioned the house, he must surely find it distressing."

"Because of the dolls?"

"Of course," the butler said with surprise, "but you are a stranger here. During the war, Georges, his only grandson, was shot while he waited for his wife, Yvette, to finish dressing for a dinner engagement. Monsieur Lambert believes she shot Georges," the butler added loyally. "And probably she did. We all thought so at the time, though she claimed that she heard someone talking to her husband in the hall."

"But she was not believed?"

"She was not credible. The Lamberts are one of the oldest families in the Var, and she was the sister of a mechanic who'd gotten rich in the black market."

I guessed that she had been unacceptable long before Georges met his end. "What happened?"

"Georges's death broke his grandfather's heart. Naturally, he pressed for a swift prosecution, but the police never found the weapon and were content to blame the shooting on those assassins in the Resistance." Though he drew himself up belligerently, ready for the fray, I was in no mood to argue French politics and let this pass. "And then Madame Lambert was Paul Desmarais's younger sister. Old families and respectable people were set aside in favor of the nouveau riche. She was completely cleared."

Desmarais kept turning up like a bad penny. "What happened to Yvette Lambert?"

"She still lives in the house. They say," the butler lowered his voice, "that she puts flowers once a month on Georges's tomb. What do you think of that?"

When I told him that was exactly what an intelligent woman would do whether she was innocent or guilty, he nodded his head sagely. "They are a treacherous family," he said. "Mechanics, all of them."

Then, as if he'd slipped on a jacket, he resumed his butler's mien, put his nose in the air, and escorted me down the corridor. I stopped for a last look at the Chavanels' miniature villa, pretty and sinister, a combination I rather like and one difficult to achieve. It was a masterpiece of sorts, and I hoped Old Lambert would take good care of it.

I found Pierre parked just at the entrance. He was looking a trifle shamefaced, as well he might. Charming as my new acquaintances were, they all favored edited versions of events. "How's the old guy?" he asked.

"Upset. His murdered grandson's wife and possible killer was Paul Desmarais's sister, so mechanics are anathema. He's proscribed your whole tribe."

"He would. Men like him are used to getting their own way, but he couldn't touch Desmarais. At one point he even suggested the Milice, not the Resistance, might be to blame, but he was smart enough not to say that too loudly."

Pierre appeared suddenly to have remembered quite a bit about the case. "But if Desmarais was so important in the Milice, would he have agreed to such a thing?"

"Paul was close to Yvette but word was that he never cared for her husband. There was some thought . . ." Pierre began and then fell silent. "The war presented opportunities," he said a moment later. "People did things they would never have done in peacetime."

I'd had an inkling of that even in London.

If Pierre was giving me the complete story, either Paul or his sister could have killed her husband, and, either way, Old Lambert might have a reason for hating mechanics. Not my worry. But if Desmarais and his sister were close, surely he would have entrusted anything of value to her, perhaps before he left the country. The business with "Madame Renard" surely meant that he was either dead or incapacitated, allowing Old Lambert to attack his daughter-in-law with impunity and Joubert to embark on some dubious scheme of his own. I thought that Yvette Lambert would be the right person to ask about a number of things, but first there was the lunch I'd promised Pierre and our return visit to the Villa Mimosa.

CHAPTER ELEVEN

I waited until we had made our way through a fine sole with cream sauce and a couple of *pichets* of the local white. Then I asked the question that had been in the back of my mind since we left the Lamberts' villa. "Old Lambert thought he recognized you, didn't he?"

Pierre shrugged, and for a moment I thought he would resume the fiction that he knew little about anything except bicycles and bike races. "He recognized my father. It still happens occasionally. We look very much alike. And a man that age would have known my father when he was young."

"He and Old Lambert were not friendly, I take it."

"My father was maybe the first mechanic to give him trouble."

A world of possibilities, but instead of elaborating Pierre

immersed himself in the dessert menu and began plumping for the lemon gâteau with ice cream on the side. By the time we had finished with little cups of espresso, a good deal of the afternoon had slipped away in the service of gastronomy, and I had reached the pleasant point where the ideal balance of alcohol and food elevates the mind beyond earthly cares.

"Do you want to see the villa?" Pierre asked.

I could think of any number of more amusing activities, but our encounter with the old man had clearly unsettled Pierre, and he looked set to be conscientious. "I can get the key from Jean-Paul at the sales office," he said and winked. What could I do but agree?

We drove in minutes up the dusty road that I had climbed so slowly in the Riviera heat, past the white houses with their bare yards and red roofs, past the little side street by the church where I had watched two men in workmen's smocks leave the villa. Pierre pulled the van to the side of the building, screened by the wall from the selectively nosy neighbors.

"As you see, Monsieur," he said in a fine estate agent voice, "this is an excellent property with adequate accommodation for all your needs. And the view, excellent."

Though my chief affection for gardens lies in their shadowed allées and secluded groves, I indicated the bare earth and dried-up plants. "The yard needs something."

"A bagatelle, Monsieur, I assure you. Any good gardener can set it right." He went on in this vein, and we were both laughing by the time he got the back door unlocked. Inside, levity stopped. We were in the stone-floored vestibule near where the late Madame Renard had come to rest after her residence in the fish locker.

I wouldn't go so far as to say that a bad spirit lingered. Without knowing the villa's history, I would have found a certain spartan charm in the place. As it was, I felt the pictorial fascination of a shadowed body against subtly modulated stones—and the chill of depression. One door led to a dusty pantry; another to the large, dark kitchen. The pantry held a bag of coffee beans, a small grinder, and a coffeepot marooned amid dusty shelves. Cooking had clearly not been high on the agenda for the two Madame Renards and their associates.

The kitchen was a similar story. A few cooking pans hung from pegs in the wall and a heavy omelet pan sat on the stove, which was old and blackened with long, but clearly not recent, use. I opened the cupboards and checked the drawers, even lifting the top of a heavy stoneware jug. Pierre waited by the sink. There was no sign of stain on the worn and uneven stones, or rather, the stains of the ages were everywhere, but both of us thought of the unfortunate "Madame Renard" and tread uneasily.

The other rooms were similarly bare of hiding places, although there was a table in what might have been the dining room, and upstairs we found four beds stripped to their springs, an ancient armoire, a cheap chest of drawers, and beside one of the beds, a night table made of rattan and surmounted by a metal lamp.

"As you see, Monsieur, all the comforts of home," Pierre said, but the joke had worn thin, and the place was making us nervous. I sat down on the bed and bounced experimentally on the metal springs.

"I'm guessing that she used this room."

He shrugged.

"What could she have left here?"

He opened the armoire, which proved empty, while I checked the drawer in the night table. Inside, I was disappointed to find only a Simenon mystery novel and a catalog of machine parts. "Eclectic reading." I held them up.

Pierre's bright face turned pale.

"What is it?"

He shook his head. "Nothing."

"You don't look like that over nothing."

He took the catalog out of my hand. It was last year's offering of various carburetors, engines, clutches, brake pads, and pistons. "This is what she left," he said.

"Why that and not the Simenon?"

"The Simenon was for fun. This was for business. Paul must have learned from Serge or maybe from one of the maquisards he interrogated."

"Enlighten me."

"It's for a form of code. If I have it right, resistants used gridded pads with random letters in each square. The key would be a line from a book that both parties owned."

Possible, I thought. Anastasie Chavanel had said that the notebook and the letter might form two-thirds of a cipher. "But how do you know it would be this particular catalog?"

"Paul never read anything but mechanical texts and parts catalogs." He thought for a minute, then said, "That is why the original Madame Renard believed the material came from him. No one else would have chosen such a thing."

"Unless Paul had nothing to do with the package. Unless Monsieur Renard is someone else entirely. Unless the package came from Joubert. He's an impresario and gambler. He'd have chosen the Simenon, whose books are easily available in both France and England."

"We take both," Pierre said, "and let the Chavanels decide. Perhaps they'll know."

"And Madame Renard. Do they know who she was? Do you?"

Pierre shook his head. "I did not recognize the photo. Truly, I did not."

I didn't necessarily believe him, but I got up from the bed and clapped him on the shoulder. "Let's get out of here. I don't think this property will suit me after all."

Pierre drove us farther up in the mountains to an abandoned farm where we took advantage of a shady half-open shed. All very exciting, though abandoned farms and stone-walled pens now come with thoughts of Richard Malet and his shallow grave, which I tried to replace with Pierre's smiling face and fine legs. He dropped me off in time for dinner. I put both books on the kitchen table.

"Well, Monsieur Francis," said Agathe. "What have we here?"

"The only personal effects left at the Villa Mimosa," I said. "Pierre favors the catalog and guesses Paul Desmarais would have picked it; I lean to the Simenon and Joubert."

"Pierre has been explaining codes and ciphers to you." She did not sound very pleased about that.

"So far as I can understand it. But all I want is my passport—and that notebook to give to Joubert. I'm not interested in what you do afterward."

"I find your lack of curiosity unrealistic."

"Tell me who the dead Madame Renard is and I'll be satisfied."

"If we knew that, we'd know exactly how to play this. But we will see what we can learn from these." Agathe tucked the books into the big pocket of her apron and took them into the workroom for her sister.

We started after dinner, or rather the aunts started. Cybèle and I were only enlisted when it became clear that there was too much material and too many possibilities. First we went line by line through the catalog and the adventures of Inspector Maigret, looking for a sentence that had been marked in some way. No luck.

"She either had a super memory or she was killed before she got an indication of the key," Anastasie concluded.

"Perhaps the key came with the letter," her sister said.

Anastasie shrugged. If the key was in the letter, we had no hope until we secured that—if it still existed. Given what I'd been told about Serge Brun, he would not have been one to hold on to a sentimental farewell message.

"What about the date?" I asked. I had been making my way through the tedious pages of the catalog, which, in addition to a dreary prose style, had its pages broken up into chapters, sections, and subsections.

"We've never seen the letter. We don't know the date," Agathe said.

"We can estimate," her sister said quickly. "Monsieur Francis said that Renard was shot early on the morning of the fifth. He would have written the letter in the next day or so. Because Francis got the package on the seventh, the date must be between those three days."

"No, I don't think that's right. Wait a minute." My visual memory is acute, and I focused on my studio, on Nan standing beside me, on the wrapper around the package, on the letter. The date was at the top. "7 March 1947," I said.

"But the date is wrong, isn't it? It can't be. Didn't you say he was shot on the morning of the fifth?"

"Right, but I can see the numbers. I remember them clearly."

"So his 'dying letter' was penned two days before he was shot." Agathe was clearly skeptical.

"Or he mistook the date, being under sedation or weak from loss of blood."

"Or else the date was deliberately chosen as a signal."

"Either is possible, but let's try 3/7/47. Are there three chapters in the parts catalog?" Agathe asked.

"There are eight chapters. And chapter three has"—I flipped through the pages— "ten sections." I turned the catalog so that everyone could see the page.

"Where is the '47'?" Agathe asked.

"There is a '4' and a '7,'" said Cybèle.

"And each of them has a parts number."

"Together they are long enough, I think, for a bank account number." Agathe wrote them down.

"Can we be sure of the order?" asked Cybèle. "I will not get more than one chance."

"We do not yet know the bank, either," Anastasie pointed out. "Trial and error will be time consuming."

"If this is from Desmarais, I guess that she would already have known the bank."

"Would she? Would he have trusted anyone but his sister?" There was discussion about this. The difficulty in dealing with people who are sly, paranoid, and untrustworthy is that they are apt to do just about anything.

"If this is from László, your Monsieur Joubert, he would know," Anastasie suggested.

"If he knew, and if Paul was dead, he would go to the bank and empty the account himself," Agathe said, which I thought was about right.

"Unless he did not understand the code. Unless he knew the bank but not how to acquire the number." That was Cybèle's contribution. "Hence his willingness to come here."

Another possibility. "So either he does not know everything or Paul isn't dead or both."

"I think Paul wrote the letter," Anastasie said. "I think he did. And Joubert either didn't notice the mistake with the date or chalked it up to Paul's state of mind."

"Right," said Cybèle. "And this Joubert thought that he would send it by Francis so that it would be easy to follow the package to Madame Renard and find the key to the message. He didn't know you were a procrastinator of the first water."

"There would be this bonus," said Agathe. "Monsieur Francis was not given good directions. He would have to ask the way to the villa. If Madame Renard was not cooperative and was injured or killed, who would be more suspicious than the foreigner who had asked directions to her house?"

"But neither one foresaw Serge," I said. "How did he get involved? How did he know about 'Madame Renard' in the first place?"

"Serge has excellent contacts in the clubs and theaters," Cybèle said, "but I don't think she was an actress or singer. I've never heard of her and at her age—"

Anastasie had another thought. "She might have been one of his Resistance contacts. An old courier or wireless operator."

"Would he have murdered someone he'd worked with?" I asked.

"He'd have murdered his mother," said Agathe.

"The woman's never been identified. Could she have been foreign?"

"Particularly if she worked the wireless," said Agathe. "Yes, I think that is possible. He would have asked her as a favor to an old comrade."

"Perhaps mentioning the Milice," her sister suggested. "Perhaps suggesting a way to settle up old scores and a way to uncover who had profited from the war."

"But we're forgetting something," Cybèle said. "Originally, Desmarais or Joubert must have had another contact in mind. There must have been a 'Madame Renard' that they had chosen."

"His sister, surely."

"Maybe. Or maybe he foresaw the danger. Maybe he had her hire someone else."

"If that's the case, we still don't know how Serge got involved."

"Right, and where is this original Madame Renard?" Cybèle asked. "One Madame Renard wound up in the fish locker, and I got away."

"Serge planned to make that escape temporary."

"Yes, he did. He wanted no witnesses."

"We need to visit Yvette Lambert," I said. "We need to find out if she is still alive."

"I think," said Agathe decisively, "that we do not know enough to act yet. You and Cybèle have been very helpful, but Anastasie and I need to concentrate now on certain details of the notebook."

So we were dismissed. I don't know how long the aunts worked, perhaps all night, because when the dawn blackbirds woke me with their fluting notes, I heard voices in the kitchen, including Cybèle, who did not strike me as an early riser. I dressed and stationed myself by the window. When I saw her leaving with a small suitcase, I slipped downstairs as quietly as I could and followed her.

I caught up with her at the first corner. "The aunts broke the rest of the cipher," I guessed.

"Not yet, but I have an engagement with a club back in Nice."

"Right, and I'm the Easter Bunny. Wherever you're off to, it sure isn't Nice. For one thing"—I nodded to the case—"you have a flat and, presumably, clothes in Nice. I'm guessing somewhere in Switzerland."

"You would be wrong. I am taking copies of the documents to Marseille for a trial."

"Marseille and then—Zurich, Geneva?"

"Who knows," she said. "But best we're not seen together."

"I thought you were estranged from the aunts, yet you're putting yourself into serious danger for them."

"Maybe I just like money," she said and stepped off briskly toward the station, her heels tapping in the morning silence.

CHAPTER TWELVE

Back to the *gare*. Fortunately, I like trains and I'm even rather fond of train stations, where once in a while fortune smiles and one meets an interesting stranger in the loo. But, today, yours truly was all business. My new passport was in my pocket, and as soon as I saw the back of Monsieur Joubert and collected the canceled gambling chits, my alter ego, Marcel Lepage, would be off for Paris and the boat train to London, where I'd be myself again and where the people who count, Nan and Arnold, would take me as I am—rowdy, promiscuous, and occasionally reckless.

Marcel, who is none of those things, had been a strain, and I would have bought the ticket and wired Arnold but for the fear of jinxing my plans. Inconspicuous behind a pillar on the eastbound platform, I brushed up on my cycling vocabulary via *Nice-Matin* until the Marseille express was announced. A rumble and a clatter, a hiss of steam, a wheeze of brakes, a clatter of doors, and Joubert, who was probably a Hungarian named László Bencze, came prancing out of one of the first-class carriages.

He was immaculately dressed in a dove gray suit, wearing a homburg and gloves, as if he were auditioning to play Hercule Poirot. "Ah, Francis," he said. "Have we a car?"

Have we wings and halos and a liveried chauffeur? "It's not a long walk," I said and led him out of the station and up the hill past the *hôtel de ville*. He complained the whole way, but though he was clearly used to being waited on, he would not let me help him with his attaché case. Interesting, that. I chose the street that fronted the house, rather than the garden entrance, which Anastasie said had been used by their wartime clients, and Joubert recognized nothing until we were at the front door and the bell was ringing deep inside.

"The Chavanels," he said, wiping his face on a silk handkerchief. "You know them?"

"One met so many people during the war," he said airily.

Anastasie opened the door, took one look at him, and said, "László Bencze. *Bonjour*. It's been a long time."

"It is all my pleasure, Madame." He made a sweeping bow without looking particularly thrilled, and when we got in the hall, he gave me a sour look. "I might have known better than to rely on you, Francis."

"You are quite wrong, there," Anastasie said. "Monsieur Francis recovered your notebook at considerable personal risk. We have merely provided a safe house for him."

Joubert bowed again without saying what he thought of this. Anastasie led him into the parlor and sent me to Agathe for some refreshments. In the kitchen, I whispered that she should beware of the attaché case. "He has something valuable or something dangerous."

"Bring that carafe of wine. We will be prepared."

I bet we would.

Back in the parlor, Anastasie had produced the notebook and demanded, bless her, my gambling chits. Joubert resisted this; he wanted the letter as well.

"You remember Serge Brun, László?" Agathe asked.

Joubert screwed up his face, miming thought.

"He was an associate of Paul Desmarais," Agathe continued. "Tall, light-brown hair, rather good-looking with a dangerous temper. Later, when Paul joined the Milice, Serge opted for the Resistance, with just about as much conviction."

"I seem to remember someone of that ilk."

"We believe that he murdered 'Madame Renard' and took both the letter and the notebook. Francis was only able to secure the notebook."

Finally, Joubert agreed to the exchange. Still looking flushed with the heat and the unaccustomed exercise, he ruffled through the pages before placing the book in his case. When Agathe came in with a tray holding wine and water bottles and some of her delicious little cakes, Joubert made another big continental bow. "Such a pleasure," he said, "to see two such charming ladies again. One had never hoped for a reunion."

"I imagine not," Agathe said dryly and passed around glasses of Chablis. "To absent comrades." Joubert raised his glass.

Anastasie took a sip of hers before asking, "And your absent comrade, Paul Desmarais? We've heard rumors of his death."

He shook his head. "As I told Francis here, there was so little hope that one assumed the end must come."

"So he's not dead," Agathe said flatly.

"He may be dead," Joubert said. "He was dying, that was certain. When I gave the package to Francis, Paul was surely dying."

"But now he has recovered?"

"Now he has disappeared." Joubert spoke in a heavy and resentful tone that reflected the sudden change in atmosphere. Planning to loot the accounts of a dead thug was one thing; going after the resources of a live one who still scared half the Var was another. "He was placed, at my expense," Joubert continued, "in a private nursing facility. He wrote the letter. Perhaps he wrote others I did not see, but he gave me the package and told me where to send it. I did not think that he would last the night, so I made the arrangements with Francis."

"A dubious arrangement," Anastasie remarked.

Joubert scowled. "I wanted it delivered in person. Who could have foreseen the death of Madame Renard?"

"Could he have left the nursing home under his own power?" Agathe wanted to know.

"Never. He had lost a tremendous amount of blood. They operated twice. Had he even been moved carelessly, he would surely be dead by now."

"But we don't know for sure, and that changes everything, does it not, László?"

"Please," he said, "I am Monsieur Joubert now." He wiped his forehead again with his fine handkerchief.

"It might be wise for you to deliver the document after all," Anastasie said.

"As you know, Madame Renard has now departed." Joubert had a strong line in euphemism.

"Who was she?"

"I only know what I was told. The package was to be sent from Monsieur Renard to Madame Renard at the Villa Mimosa."

"Not to his sister?"

He shook his head and wiped his face again. Back with acquaintances from the heroic days, Joubert did not seem like the hectoring and confident gambling impresario he was in London.

"Who else would he trust?" Anastasie asked.

"You ladies would know better than I."

"Nonsense. You've had associates in town. You've seen the photos. Who was she?"

Joubert hesitated, thinking this over. I began to doubt that he did anything spontaneously. "I believe that she was a refugee," he said after a minute. "East European, possibly Jewish. Paul noticed her when she was detained by the Milice. She needed papers, a safe place to stay."

"Though we never saw her," Anastasie said. "We made no papers for such a person."

"No. By that time he was a big shot in the Milice and did not wish to be compromised by working with you. He made some arrangements; she survived the war. She owed him a big favor."

"It cost her life," I said. "And it's kept her from being identified."

Joubert nodded. "There is always a risk with valuable shipments."

Another philosopher at someone else's expense. "It might have been me," I said.

Joubert's expression suggested that I would be no loss.

Agathe spoke up. "Well, Monsieur Whoever-You-Are-Now, I think our business is complete. You have your document, Monsieur Francis has his gambling chits returned. My sister and I have work to do." She stood up.

Joubert picked up his attaché case and balanced it on his knees. "A moment, Madame."

"Yes?"

"You and your sister surely know that this material is valuable."

"It is not ours, Monsieur."

"Please, do not insult my intelligence. You will know as well as I do why Paul sent it: He was dying or believed he was and wished to get valuable information into trusted hands and ultimately to his sister."

"The more reason to deliver the notebook to Madame Lambert."

"Paul had a gambling habit and owed me money. He is dead or incapacitated. Either way, unless I help myself, I'm unlikely to be paid. Besides, who owns such money? He seized what he could; he held it while he was able. Now—" He shrugged. "I suspect you've had the same thought."

"The material is cryptic," said Anastasie. "That Paul Desmarais is, or was, wealthy is not in dispute. How your package secures that money is not clear to me."

Joubert put his hand in his case and came out with a pistol. Military surplus certainly has a lot to answer for. "Dear ladies," he said, "you have had several days to work on the problem. I do not believe our friend Paul was clever enough to have defeated you. Letter or no letter, I need to know where Paul has stashed his fortune."

The sisters exchanged a look. "Be set to be disappointed," Agathe said. "You are right. We assume the material forms a sort of cipher. But the loss of the letter is one problem. The other is that Paul didn't trust anyone completely, and the key is missing."

"Would Madame Renard have had it?"

Anastasie shrugged. They really were a cool pair. "Perhaps. Or perhaps his sister. Without the key, and perhaps the letter, the notebook is without value. Like that weapon, Monsieur."

"You would say the same if you had found the key and worked out the solution," Joubert observed.

I'm not sure the sisters noticed, but I could see Joubert's pistol waver slightly. Of course, being a good deal heavier than me, the drug probably acted more slowly on him.

"You are quite right, dear László, so you must decide which is more probable. And which is less dangerous, to do something irrevocable to us or to assume Paul is alive and collect your gambling debts in some other way."

Without putting down the pistol, Joubert wiped his forehead again with his silk handkerchief. "I am no longer used to this charming climate," he said.

The old ladies said nothing but sat watching him as still as cats. All of a sudden, he lurched to his feet, the attaché case tumbled to the floor, and the pistol discharged into the ceiling. Joubert collapsed into the chair, his eyes closed, his face flushed. The weapon slipped from his grasp, and I picked it up.

"I hope he's not had some sort of attack." I didn't fancy helping the police with any new inquiries.

Agathe laid her hand on his chest. "We should have given him more," she said. "What's in the case?"

Anastasie investigated. "Nothing much. A change of underwear and socks, the notebook, of course, and an address book. A few names here in the Var, we will copy those, and a train reservation for Zurich. We are making progress, Monsieur Francis."

She went into the kitchen and emerged with a bottle of beer and a small bottle of brandy.

"What about Joubert? He has friends here. They will probably know that he was meeting me."

"But not where. That was well done, Monsieur Francis. And now we will stage a little comedy. Help me take him to the foyer."

We each took an arm, levered the heavy Joubert from his chair, and half walked and half dragged him through to the tiled foyer, where Anastasie sprinkled him lavishly with a mix of brandy and beer and left him, as she put it, "to percolate" for a while. He started stirring at dusk, and Agathe and I got him out of the house by the rear entrance and deposited him with the precious briefcase just outside one of the restaurants in the upper town.

"Monsieur Leclerc! Monsieur Leclerc!" Agathe called.

When the proprietor came out, formal in a dull black tuxedo, and looking gray and anxious, she exclaimed about the drunken man in the street. "A scandal, Monsieur. That he is in such a state." And so on.

Monsieur Leclerc, in turn, grew incensed at the idea that this *étranger* had been in his establishment. "But no, Madame Chavanel. But never!"

They raised their voices and argued back and forth across Joubert, who had lost all his usual elegance to slump drooling on the pavement. Aunt Agathe and Monsieur Leclerc seemed genuinely excited and upset, but their responses were so pat that I concluded they had used the routine before. They carried on until the café patrons, the waiters, even the cooks had been alerted and the windows of the neighboring houses were thrown open; then Monsieur Leclerc drew himself up and announced that, purely as a humane and public-spirited gesture, he would summon the gendarmes.

"Poor man," Agathe said, her indignation vanishing. "I know he will be in good hands with you, Monsieur Leclerc." She took my arm and we walked back to the house.

"He will remember," I said.

"When he remembers, it will be too late. And you, Monsieur. You would do well now to leave as soon as possible."

I thought that good advice.

CHAPTER THIRTEEN

Debt free and carrying excellent papers, I was set to leave the golden Riviera. I had collected thanks from the Chavanels, busy packing for what Anastasie described as a "strategic holiday." I had abandoned my former passport and gifted the remains of my sketching kit to a beachfront rival. There was nothing to keep me from a speedy return home, where I'd see Nan and go to bed with Arnold and get into my studio. I was bound for the post office to telegraph the good news, when someone called, "Francis."

I'd make a terrible spy, a dreadful double agent. Forgetting Monsieur Lepage, I turned around to see Pierre, waving frantically. "I could do with a hand," he said.

Ordinarily, nothing would please me more, but the afternoon

express, the through connection from Marseille to Paris, and the boat train awaited, as well as a resolution to behave with prudence and common sense.

"Another delivery," Pierre said. "We can take the motorcycle."

I explained my travel plans and hinted at the necessity for leaving town immediately.

"Perfect. You can take the night train from Cannes and avoid the station here—if you need to."

That remark should have told me something right there, but I guess "prudence and common sense" don't necessarily include intelligence. "I'm afraid it will have to be a modest dinner," I said, as most of Malet's cash would go for tickets.

"I know a place by the docks. Very good, very cheap."

How quickly other considerations vanish in the face of food and drink with a handsome companion. We walked to the bike shop, where I was once again wedged into the sidecar with various bicycle parts. Outside Cannes, we met up with a bicycle support truck, where Pierre delivered gears and brakes to a group of thin, intense men in black bike shorts and bright shirts, who discussed gear adjustments, brake tension, and other arcane technical matters like monks with a psalter. It was dusk before we made our way to a sailors' bistro where the tide slapped at the pilings beneath the floor. The fish only came fried but it was fresh, and the bread and soup were excellent. Pierre entertained me with the progress of the Tour, while I revealed as little as possible about my adventures with the Chavanels.

Everything was fine, more than fine, until we decided to have a wander on one of the beaches before I was delivered to the train station. For reasons that you can imagine, we picked one beyond the city lights, and we were cruising along on our way to pleasure and the *plage*, when a vehicle ran up behind us in a loud and aggressive way, flooding the sidecar with light. I expected him to overtake us, probably with more élan than sense. An oncoming car passed us, then two more. With the road ahead clear, the car accelerated and drew level. I saw a glint of metal in the open back window, shouted to Pierre, and slid down as far as I could in the sidecar. There was an explosion; Pierre hit the brakes; the motorcycle slewed left and right, bounced off the back end of the sedan, caromed across the road, banged into a low retaining wall then angled over both lanes, jumped the curb, and flew onto the sand.

I found myself dangling at a crazy angle, enveloped in the smell of hot oil and distressed metal, with my shoulders inches above the cool, gray beach. Another lurch and the sidecar came to rest while the cycle, still game, threw up a volcano of sand.

"Get out, get out!" Pierre cried. I saw him tumble off the bike and crouch behind the half-upended sidecar.

Something pinged off the metal, and I slithered out to join him. More shots, two or three at least, before the lights of oncoming traffic sent the car accelerating away. Pierre stood up and occupied himself with French invective, while I moved various parts of my anatomy to see whether everything that was burning and aching was still operational.

"They will be back," I suggested finally, which set Pierre to poking and probing, first the sidecar, which had a shot-out tire and a serious list, then the cycle itself, which, with encouragement, ground its motor and showed signs of life. He took a wrench from the little pannier that held his tools and loosened the bolts holding the sidecar, abandoning it on the shore. With that weight removed, we wrestled the motorcycle out of the sand and hauled it up onto firmer ground.

Though I was concerned that our attackers would return, Pierre refused to abandon the valuable bike, and I did not feel that I could leave when I'd brought him so much trouble. He wheeled the motorcycle under a streetlight well off the main road and set to work. At last, he got the motor running properly and hopped on.

"I can walk," I said. "You go back. I'll find my own way to the *gare*."

He pointed out the dangers of this, and we were arguing back and forth when we heard a car. Just an ordinary car to me, but the mechanic's ear detected something more ominous. "Get on the back," he cried, and before I was well seated, he gunned the motor, which accelerated despite sand and salt to carry us away from the shore—and the station. Up in the older part of town, Pierre plunged into a network of small streets, cornering recklessly and weaving between cars.

"Are they behind us?"

I strained to see over my shoulder. The lights of a dark car bobbed several vehicles behind us. Pierre made a sharp turn; seconds later, the sedan followed. "Yes," I said. "Yes." I thought perhaps I could get off, that with less weight the cycle would move faster, that Pierre would be safer alone. But when I shouted for him to let me off, he refused. "They want us both," he said, which opened other possibilities and, with a cry of "hang on," he took an alley that would have been too narrow for the sidecar and which stymied our pursuers. He wove between the litter bins and scraped back stoops to emerge at a street bordering a park. The motorcycle roared up a steep hill into a leafy residential area that looked respectable and dark. Here the valiant machine began to stutter and wheeze, and I became aware of a strong smell of petrol.

"I think the tank is leaking," I shouted, his curly hair blowing against my mouth. "We're running out of gas."

Pierre slowed up, trying to nurse the motor just a little farther, but it sputtered to a halt, and we jumped off. When Pierre spotted a driveway running between high walls, he wheeled the bike behind some cypress trees. My impulse was to walk back to the *gare*, but the sound of a heavy car cruising on the street beyond sent us running up the drive. The windows of the villa were all dark, but something about the silhouette against the night sky was familiar, and as we crept down the side toward the garden, the long windows, decorative trim, and cornice all came into focus. I realized that I was looking at the original of the Chavanels' masterly miniature.

"This is Madame Lambert's house," I said and grabbed his arm. "Did you know?"

"Only now," Pierre said.

For the moment, I chose to believe him.

The back garden was a fine one, laid out in geometric beds and surrounded by more of the funereal cypresses. I fancied a moonlit evening there, but the car nosed up the drive, and we fled to the terrace, where, more in desperation than hope, I tried one of the French doors. It opened without a sound. Pierre stepped inside and I followed, locking the door behind us.

All quiet within. An open window cast a rectangle of moonlight on the floor and a curtain moved slightly in the night breeze. Otherwise only a few thin bars of light crept though the shutters. We settled ourselves behind an overstuffed couch and waited. A voice in the garden, footsteps on the terrace, a door latch being jiggled—all bad things, followed by whispers. *They know we're here,* I thought, and I expected the crack of glass and the speedy entrance of our pursuers. But no, the voices receded. A minute later, I went to the French doors and peered out. The terrace was empty, the garden deserted. They had just been guessing, and they might go on to try every drive and every garden on the street.

"Pierre," I said.

No answer. I became aware that the house had a slightly musty, closed-up smell as if no one lived here, although the rear door had been left unlocked and a window open. Now that our immediate danger had receded, I felt disturbance like a lingering shock wave. I walked down the long tiled corridor toward the front of the house. On my right would be the library and the dining room; on my left, the best parlor with the ancestor portrait over the mantel and a frescoed ceiling. It was curious to see the house come to life, shooting up, as it were, from its doll-sized prototype. Pierre was standing beside the elegant curving stairs where, supposedly, Madame Lambert had shot her husband.

"Don't touch anything," he warned.

"What is it?" I asked, but even in the dimness, I saw the shape on the floor, a woman with long hair in a dark dress. "Is it Madame Lambert?"

"I'm guessing." He put his hand on her neck and immediately drew back as if startled.

"Is she alive?" I stepped forward ready to put my ARP training to use.

"She is cold," said Pierre. "She is like ice."

"The fish locker."

"Serge Brun," he said.

I did not have time to digest this idea, for in the distance we heard the sound of a police Klaxon. I could see myself providing assistance to the French police until I had gray hair. "Let's get out of here," I said. In my anxiety, I must have raised my voice, for a cry came from the upper floor.

"Who is it? Who is there?"

We both jumped. When we came back down to earth, we saw a shadow above and the foyer lights came on. A woman with auburn hair and a distraught expression on her pale freckled face ran half-way downstairs and stopped. She was wearing a summer dress and carrying an old shotgun. I'm not sure I like Frenchwomen's taste in accessories.

"Who are you?" she demanded, her voice rising. "Don't move or I'll call the police."

"Don't shoot. We won't hurt you," Pierre said.

"What has happened? Why are you here? You aren't friends of Madame's."

"Some men attacked us. We ran into your garden and found the rear door open."

"How was that possible, Monsieur? I locked up as usual. Eight thirty, I lock the garden door."

"I think whoever brought this," Pierre gestured toward the body. With the lights up, I could see that the dead woman's hair was dark blond, her face, well preserved rather than youthful. "Can you get a sheet or a blanket?"

She took a step closer, night in her eyes. "Oh, no! Oh, no! Has he killed Madame?"

"We don't know who she is," I said.

She came down to the last step, looked at the body, and raised the shotgun at us. "Oh, poor Madame Lambert ! My poor Madame Lambert! Don't move," she cried, then turned and fled upstairs with a little gasp. Pierre started to follow her, but I put my hand on his arm and shook my head. "Give her a moment."

Sure enough, she reappeared, still with the gun but now wearing a thin coat and carrying both a purse and a bundle of linen. She came downstairs and covered the body gently. "She is so cold! Poor thing! Her arm is like ice." She stood, clutching her weapon and visibly shivering.

I didn't feel too good myself. I touched one of her thin shoulders. "When did you last see your employer?"

"How do I know it wasn't you?" she asked, moving away angrily and raising the shotgun again. "Who are you? How did you get in here?"

She went on in this vein, until Pierre introduced me as Marcel Lepage, visiting decorator—"Quite famous, madam!"—and himself as a member of the Sud-Est racing team. I noticed that he was careful not to give his name, but his explanation was apparently adequate, for when I asked a second time about the dead woman, she answered.

"Tuesday it was. There was a terrible argument. He arrived just at lunch."

"Who? Who arrived?"

"Monsieur Brun."

"Serge Brun?" Pierre asked.

"You know him?" She gave Pierre a sharp glance. "Yes, that is his name. I had just brought in the soufflé when he rang the bell. I brought him into the dining room."

"He was a welcome visitor, who came often?"

"He was not welcome to me, Monsieur, but Madame said that he was an old friend. Lately, he had come often. More often than I liked." Though she was still trembling, her voice was firm. Her slight, almost girlish form had deceived me. I realized that she was at least as old as her late employer.

"You said there was an argument."

"Something he wanted—as usual. I didn't catch the details, but she was furious. Really furious. Then he showed her something, a piece of paper." She was silent for a moment.

"And then?" Pierre prompted.

"Then she ordered him out of the house, Monsieur. It was quite a scene. Marie will remember."

"Who is Marie?"

"She comes in to cook whenever Madame is home."

"You said you hadn't seen Madame Lambert since Tuesday. When did she leave?"

"That afternoon, Monsieur. She packed a small bag and called a taxi. And now here she is and so cold. How is she so cold, Messieurs?"

Pierre and I exchanged glances. "She has perhaps been kept somewhere cold," I suggested, though I couldn't bring myself to mention the fish locker.

"We must call the police," she said and moved toward the back of the foyer where, I now saw, there was a telephone on a small gilt table. That was one detail the Chavanels had missed but perhaps it was a recent addition. "The police must know. They know she has enemies." She leaned the shotgun against a table and lifted the receiver.

We moved toward the door.

"A moment, Messieurs, if you please. How did you get here?"

We explained about the motorcycle.

"I have a better idea," she said. "But first, I must call the police."

She dialed the number, then turned her back on us and spoke to the officer on duty, demanding to be contacted with the chief inspector. "I am calling about Madame Yvette Lambert."

A pause, then she gave a swift but accurate description of the victim and instructed the officers to use the unlocked terrace entrance. She had a rather imperious manner for a personal maid, and I was surprised at how crisp and decisive she sounded, especially when she said, "Certainly, the victim is Madame Lambert. And you will know who is to blame, Inspector. "

I didn't have time to consider the oddities of this conversation, for as soon as she hung up the telephone, she took a set of keys from a small bureau and motioned for us to follow her. We went out by the terrace, and, though I may have been deceived in the moonlight, I thought that she did something with the door latch. We walked beside the garden wall to a stone garage with a nice Peugeot sedan inside. Pierre got behind the wheel, she got into the backseat, still with the shotgun, and I closed up the garage doors and slid in beside Pierre. We crossed the gravel sweep in front of the villa and headed down the drive.

"We can drop Marcel at the *gare*," Pierre suggested, and he signaled for a right turn.

"We're going together," she said and she laid the shotgun against his ear. "All of us."

"Marcel is just a visitor," Pierre said.

"A pity," she said. "You chose the wrong house and the wrong time, Monsieur." And she moved the shotgun in my direction.

"I am surprised you did not want to wait and assist the police, Mademoiselle—how awkward we do not yet know your name."

"Pelletier," she said.

"Have you worked for Madame Lambert for a long time?"

"Forever," she said. "But you see what has happened to my poor Madame. There is not much point in my going the same way, is there?"

"None at all. Yet you are well protected." I nodded toward the shotgun, which she seemed to handle with a good deal of confidence. How many personal maids go shooting?, I wondered, though Nan had more than once picked up a hunting rifle during the Irish Troubles of my childhood, when we cowered in the big basement kitchen, alert for shouts and torches outside.

She did not answer, but directed Pierre to take the main coastal road east. "Do not think of leaving the vehicle," she told me. "I will shoot him without hesitation."

I knew then and perhaps Pierre guessed, too.

I turned around and looked at her. "Very well, Madame Lambert," I said.

CHAPTER FOURTEEN

Yvette Lambert with her brightly dyed hair and now unconcealed arrogance directed Pierre to the coastal road toward Nice, then up into the dark hills, an itinerary that provoked bad thoughts and bad memories. As the lights of the city diminished and the rail line with my exit route slipped away behind us, I glanced at Pierre, but he just shrugged and focused on the roads, which became steadily rougher and narrower.

I wondered whether we had a better chance to survive ignorant or knowledgeable. As far as the gun-toting Madame Lambert knew, I was Marcel Lepage, decorator. Unless she had something against Pierre, we were simply annoyances with reasons of our own for avoiding the police. On the other hand, her associates seemed very fond of using the fish locker.

Would my undeniable assistance to her brother soften her heart? Though I was tempted to conjure up Victor Renard's shooting for her, I didn't feel I could go that far without consulting Pierre, and I was still worrying this question when we entered an unpaved track. I had the nasty thought that we were returning to the abandoned farm where Cybèle and I had buried the late Richard Malet, but this farmhouse, if ancient, was well roofed and solid with a variety of stone outbuildings. An oil lamp was burning in one window. Madame Lambert directed Pierre toward what might have been a stable and told him to shut off the motor and leave the keys in the car.

The door of the house opened, and two men with flashlights approached. One was the balding chap I had seen at the Villa Mimosa. Proximity revealed a fleshy face with a little cupid's bow mouth and small eyes sunk on either side of a thick nose. The other was a tall, fair man with an angular jaw and mean eyes who could have passed for English or German. Pierre whispered, "Serge Brun."

"Get out of the car," Brun said, "and put your hands on the hood."

We did as we were told. The bald man searched us, removing my wallet. I regretted the loss of Malet's francs and even more the little scraps of paper with his handwriting on them. Were Brun to recognize them, what was dangerous might turn catastrophic.

"I warned you to be discreet," he told Yvette, his voice harsh. "I warned you to involve no one else. Who are these men?"

"They walked in the open terrace door, saw the body, and asked a lot of questions. Had you followed my instructions, they would probably still be hiding in the garden." She spoke calmly, indifferent to his anger.

"And now you want me to tidy up the mess," he shouted. "You must think I'm a garbage collector."

"I think you are willing to do whatever is required."

They glared at each other for a few seconds, before he turned away. That was interesting, but she was still holding the shotgun in a knowledgeable way. "Tie them up and take them inside," he yelled to the bald man. "We'll deal with them."

None of this sounded good to me. Fun and games in dark places can be entertaining, but not at the back of beyond among people with complex politics. The bald man tied our hands behind our backs and pushed us through the darkness toward the building. When Pierre stumbled on the step and fell, the man kicked him hard in the ribs. Without thinking, I kicked him behind his left knee, catching him off balance so that he dropped his light and wound up on his hands and knees on the step. Mistake. He got up in a fury and struck me on the side of the face. When I staggered back against the house, he hit me again, and I was in line for serious damage, when Yvette shouted, "Victor! Victor! You idiot."

The flashlight lying on the ground illuminated his features from below, picking out anger and something else that might have been pleasure. I tasted blood in my mouth and realized this could be worse than I'd imagined. He jerked Pierre to his feet, picked up the flashlight, and threw open the door. An archway on the left led to a kitchen. The main room with a stone fireplace was straight ahead, lit by a single oil lamp hanging from the ceiling. The foyer was empty except for a chair and a heavy wooden door set into the right-hand wall. Victor pushed us against this, and Brun shone his flashlight directly in our faces. He took a good look and didn't seem pleased with what he saw.

"What were you doing in the garden?"

"Hiding," I said.

Pierre added that we had been chased there.

Brun struck him heavily in his injured side, and Pierre screamed, his face white with pain.

"It's true," I said. "We ran into some tough types near the port. There was an argument."

He cracked me across the mouth. "Sure. And you ran all the way across Cannes."

I spit out blood. "We had Pierre's motorbike. Which was damaged and ran out of gas. We hid it in the driveway and ran into the garden."

He didn't believe us. "You asked questions." And he struck my ribs with his flashlight so that my breath seized up with pain.

"We walked in an open door and found a woman lying dead on the floor and someone with a shotgun. That's not normal décor."

This time he hit me hard enough so that I momentarily lost the light. From some distant constellation I heard him shout, "How did you know it was Madame Lambert? How did you know that?"

This question was trouble. Don't mention the dollhouse, which would lead to the Chavanels, which would lead to Cybèle and codes and things I'd better not remember. Don't mention Victor Renard, whom my alter ego Marcel did not know. "She didn't seem like a lady's maid." I'd had some teeth loosened and the words came out a mumble.

Yvette Lambert laughed at this, but she hoisted the shotgun in a menacing way, and Brun relieved his feelings by cracking Pierre's shoulder with his flashlight. I believe that things would have gone seriously downhill, if Victor hadn't yelled, "Quiet!" and run to the doorway. Now we all heard the rumble of a vehicle approaching along the rough track. He closed the heavy outer door, as Brun shoved us to one side and opened the cellar. Swinging at both of us with his flashlight, he forced us onto the top of a steep stairway and tumbled us down. Pierre gave a cry as his bruised side hit the stone steps. I went head over heels, bounced on my head, bashed my arm and shoulder, and wound up facedown on a dirt floor that smelled of old vegetables. Above, the door rattled and banged shut.

The back of my head throbbed, and red and green constellations wheeled across my retinas until I gradually got myself located in space. When I felt my knees under me, I levered myself upright. One elbow was touching the bottom of the stone stairs, and I managed to crawl onto the lowest step. No sound from Pierre, which worried me as I was sure I had been out for some minutes.

"Pierre. You all right?"

A sound in front of me. Pierre wheezed a little as he answered, "Just my ribs."

"Could that be the gendarmes arriving?"

"A nice thought, but unlikely." I heard him moving slowly toward the steps. "Can you untie me?"

My hands were tied so tightly that they were already half numb, but I found the knot on Pierre's bonds and began picking at it. A few minutes later, my fingers were bleeding but Pierre was beginning to move his hands.

"I've got it now," he said.

I heard him moving his arms and rubbing his hands. Then he set to work on the rope around my wrists. "Don't drop the ropes. They're all we have."

"Not much good against a shotgun," Pierre said.

"There's the element of surprise. I'll bet there's no electric light down here."

Pierre laughed. "No electricity period in these old farmhouses."

"Well, then."

He thought this over. "One of us stands at the top of the stairs and garrotes whoever opens the door?"

This was a bolder plan than I'd have devised, but I could see its attractions. Pierre was clearly a man of talent, and the war had developed his abilities quite a bit further than my ARP unit had mine. "Wouldn't the others hear?"

Pierre allowed that this might be the case and finished untangling the rope around my wrists; I began to feel that my hands were once again attached to my body.

"What about one of us lying at the foot of the stairs and luring him down?"

"You don't want to be in the line of fire. We must see if there is a place to hide," he said.

I heard him moving in the darkness, touching the stairs, feeling for the back wall. I began to do the same. We were in a fairly large space, and the darkness was disorienting. We'd have had difficulties finding the stairs again but for the sliver of light under the door above. "A *cave*," Pierre said. "For storing wine."

"Vegetables, too, I'd guess." I'd touched some earth-filled boxes—shades of the grave. I hoped that raw earth would not continue to remind me of Richard Malet's final resting place.

"If they both come down, we're finished," Pierre said. "Brun will shoot without hesitation. He might anyway."

"Lovely chap. What about Victor? He didn't do much of a job tying us up."

"The woman maybe wants some answers. I'm not sure about Brun and his buddy."

"I have some answers for her," I said, "but not as Marcel Lepage."

"Don't think of it. If they suspect you were at the villa or that you know anything about the notebook or codes, they'll just open the door and blast away. It wouldn't be the first time."

I suddenly didn't like the idea of being the decoy. "We must make them come down," I said, but I could hear Pierre moving up the stairs, and before we could argue the point, there were sounds loud enough to penetrate even the thick walls of the cellar. I stepped around the side of the stairs as the door was thrust open with an explosion of light. A silhouette, a man in the doorway, and a deafening bang set my brain vibrating. Then the light diminished with the sound of the door thrust against a body. A shout and some-one somersaulted down the stairs. The shotgun landed several feet away from me. I made a lunge for it, kicking at the figure sprawled on the dirt, seized the weapon by the barrel, and swung it at the man's head and shoulder.

Pierre stepped into the light of the doorway. Although still deafened, I could see that he was shouting, and I ran up the steps. Clearly something had happened while we were immured below. The oil lamp was out, the front door was open, and outside I could see more car lights than there should have been. I ran into the kitchen where Pierre threw open the rear door. We plunged into a rampant tangle of weeds, herbs, and shrubs, rounded the back of the farmhouse, and sprinted behind the barns.

From our new vantage point, we saw Yvette's car, the big black fish truck, and another large sedan with its lights on and both its front doors open, as if the passengers had stepped out without closing them. There was something on the ground, a large shape, maybe two, and I had just registered these when Pierre grabbed my shoulder and pulled me back. I caught a glimpse of figures run-ning, then I followed Pierre along a stone-walled paddock and into the fields, where I fell twice before we finally took shelter behind a large rock surrounded by scrub.

We lay on the ground, listening to the whirr and hum of night insects and our own labored breathing. I had a tooth loose, my mouth hurt, and an assortment of bruises combined with the stony ground made any comfort impossible.

"Will they follow us, do you think?"

"Not now. There were shots; they will leave. And deal with us later. Or contrive to blame us."

I didn't like the sound of that.

"Nothing to do until morning," Pierre said and fell silent. Eventually I must have fallen asleep, too, because when he touched my shoulder, the sky had lightened to the east and the farthest hills were outlined against a wash of pearly gray.

"We should start now," he said, his voice cracked and hoarse. "We might catch a farm truck heading to the coast."

I found that I could barely speak myself, and as soon as I moved, I discovered bruises unsuspected the night before. "We need water."

Pierre stood up and surveyed the rough countryside. "There will be paths, but I don't know this area. I think we should go back," he said.

"And if Brun and Company are in residence?"

"We make a swift retreat."

I couldn't think of a better plan. We thrust our way through the scrub to the shelter of the stable and other outbuildings. Everything was quiet. The fish locker truck and Madame Lambert's handsome Peugeot were nowhere in evidence, although the large sedan with the open doors was still parked in front of the building. There was a steady hum of flies in the morning air, and as we drew closer, a throat-catching stench, lightly tinctured with gunpowder. Two bodies were on the ground. The driver had a thin face with a low forehead punctured by a blackening wound. The other man was heavy with the brutal features I remembered from our conversation in the café and dark stains on his shirt and trousers.

"Do you recognize them?"

"The bigger man talked to me. He wanted Joubert's notebook back. We had dinner on his tab."

"I recognize the Renault—it's one of the new rear engine 4CVs. They tracked us to Madame Lambert's, and they must have hung around the neighborhood and followed her car."

"Lucky for us."

We went to the farmhouse. The door was locked, but after a

little searching we located a well with a pump and a bucket outside the stable. We drank as much as we could and washed the blood off our faces and hands. Pierre looked slightly less pale, but I noticed that he was walking with difficulty.

"It's miles to town, isn't it?"

"I've done harder in worse shape on the bike."

Right. Cyclists are deeply conversant with pain and endurance. I had hoped to be less knowledgeable. "What about their car?"

"We're already going to be suspicious."

"As Nan says, might as well be hanged for a sheep as a lamb. Besides, they ruined your motorbike."

Pierre considered this for a moment. "What about them?"

"We could bury them," I said, though I dreaded the exertion.

"You surprise me, Francis."

"Marcel, please."

"Very well."

He proved to be more of a country person than Cybèle. After a little reconnoitering, he located what had been an old manure pit. I found this a distasteful idea, but when I lifted the first shovelful of the soft compost, my reservations disappeared. Within an hour, we had removed all trace of our two pursuers. Pierre pumped another bucket of water and cleaned the side of the car. We could do nothing about the bullet holes at the moment.

He got into the driver's seat and tried the engine. A cough, a grunt, and then a very satisfactory low rumble. "Hop in," said Pierre. "We're getting out of here."

"Have we a destination?"

"We're going to see Hector. He knew Paul, Brun, and the Lamberts in the old days, the Chavanels, too."

"And what does he do?"

"He was a commandant with the Sûreté Nationale."

"A policeman. Pierre, we've just finished not one but two illicit burials."

"He *was* a policeman. Based in Nice. When the Italians moved in, he went to the hills. He's the man who can help us."

I wasn't sure about that. My experience with London coppers has been almost uniformly negative, and Inspector Chardin had finished my enthusiasm for the French variety.

"Have you got a better idea?" Pierre asked.

Let's see: We were banged up like third-rate boxers, we were flat broke, pursued by folk with a sideline in homicide, and driving a car belonging to two dead thugs. "Not at the moment," I said.

CHAPTER FIFTEEN

Hector lived near Antibes, Picasso territory, the locale of bimorphs disporting on the beach, home of cubist gods and goddesses. The great man clearly had happier times on the Mediterranean than I'd had so far. But then joie de vivre isn't exactly my subject, and I had to admit that there was plenty going on to feed my particular pictorial obsessions. Perhaps Hector would provide more of the same, for Pierre assured me that he had been formidable at laying explosives and planning ambushes. "He is a man to trust with your life," Pierre said, which was more than I could say for most of my associates.

This remarkable character lived in a small white stucco house next to a patisserie and a *tabac*; Pierre pulled smartly into the alley alongside. Hector's place sported a pair of fancy urns holding a variety of bright flowers, and the low façade was ornamented with window boxes of geraniums. I wonder if retired coppers routinely turned to horticulture, if all that pruning, pinching, and deadheading console them after careers of nipping crime in the bud.

Pierre knocked, and the door opened almost immediately—Hector was clearly an early riser who kept his perimeter under observation. Small but trim, he had a military bearing that reminded me unpleasantly of my father, fine features, still dark hair swept straight back, and deeply tanned skin over high cheekbones. Behind his horn-rimmed glasses, his eyes were black and faintly slanted, which combined with the neatness of his person to give him an almost Asiatic appearance. I found it hard to imagine him on the operating end of a machine gun, but I was soon to discover that he was a man who could turn his hand to whatever was required.

"Pierre, Pierre! I hadn't expected to see you until the next Criterion. You'll be riding, I hope." But even as he spoke, his voice took on a doubtful tone. He'd noticed the bruises on Pierre's face, a certain stiffness in his stance, and our general dishevelment.

"Nothing serious. Ribs," he said.

"Come in, and your friend, too."

"Marcel Lepage," Pierre said.

Something, perhaps Hector's air of rectitude and competence, impelled me to add, "At the moment."

"Ah, a *nom de guerre*. Now that takes me back."

"Back is where we need to go, Hector," Pierre said. The older man's face assumed a curious new expression, at once still and watchful, and he led us into a small bright kitchen with modern appliances and a big square table. "Sit. We'll have coffee. And maybe croissants? I find excursions into the past require sustenance."

We couldn't conceal how hungry we were, and Hector followed

up the croissants with a fine baguette and some cheese. "We didn't get breakfast."

"Owing to a rapid departure," Pierre added.

"Under fire, perhaps?" Hector nodded back toward the window. "I noticed the Renault."

Pierre allowed that the Renault had taken a hit.

"And its occupant?"

Pierre and I exchanged glances.

"Gone to ground," I said. "Both of them."

Hector looked at us as if he could see all the way back to the old farm and our stint of dawn grave digging. "We need not worry about them?"

"Definitely not," said Pierre. "I think they will not be found for some time."

"But we're still in a pickle."

"I can't help if I don't know," Hector said.

Pierre took a deep breath and gave a rapid account of the night's events, beginning with the attack near the beach and continuing with our adventures accompanying Madame Lambert in the hinterland. I saw a new side of him as he spoke. The boyish and amusing cyclist disappeared and someone else, older, wearier, sharper appeared. He was cool and accurate and gave no more information than was required.

"Well," Hector said. "You do take me back: Serge Brun, Yvette Lambert, and possible associates of László Bencze. An eventful evening to be sure. But, Pierre, this cannot be connected with the war. You had nothing to do with Brun, and László had already fled for parts unknown when you joined our group." He turned to me and said, "Pierre was our youngest recruit. He was delivering messages for us while he was still in short pants."

Pierre smiled for the first time. "Race training was a good cover."

"Yes, and it made you a cyclist." Hector gave him an affectionate glance. I could see that he was genuinely fond of my friend.

"I'm afraid Pierre's present trouble is all my fault. I saw a man named Victor Renard shot outside a London gambling club owned by Monsieur Joubert—whom you knew as László Bencze." I described Renard's injuries, my probably futile attempts to stop the bleeding, and my errand to deliver Renard's "last words" to Madame Renard.

"Poor Madame Renard," he said. "You were perhaps the last to see her?"

"I did not see her at all." I recounted my visit to the villa and most of the subsequent events, omitting only my work for the Chavanels and my adventure with Cybèle.

"A turbulent holiday," he remarked when I'd finished. "And difficult to accomplish if the police have your passport." He gave me a shrewd look.

"I was able to acquire an identity card. Hence my new persona, Marcel Lepage."

"Might I see it?"

I glanced at Pierre, who nodded.

"Very nice," Hector said after he had run a connoisseur's eye over the card. "The workmanship is very fine—and familiar. Old friends of mine made this for you. Am I right?"

"I don't know who your old friends might be."

"Charming ladies."

"Then it would be ungallant to involve them."

He laughed at this. "They survived the war on skill, charm, and guile. They and the most attractive Cybèle."

"I'm afraid that she is in danger. The Chavanels know a good deal more than is healthy, and though the old ladies have supposedly gone on vacation, I believe that Cybèle is off to make her fortune."

"With Renard's mysterious notebook?"

"More or less. She said that she was taking a copy of the notebook to the authorities in Marseille."

Hector nodded at this. "She would do that. You can trust the ladies to put any evidence in the right hands."

"I am glad to hear that, but the Chavanels also seem to know a good deal about codes and ciphers."

"They do, indeed." He smiled. "It would be poetic justice if they were able to access Paul's fortune."

"Except we are not even sure Victor Renard is Paul Desmarais or that he is really dead."

"It would take a lot to kill Paul, but that he was calling himself Victor Renard is a sure thing."

"Why is that?"

"The name, for one thing."

"The Chavanels thought it was a message from Cybèle."

Hector shook his head. "No, though it is connected with them, too." He went into the front room and returned with a bulging folder of papers. "I retired during the war; unofficially, I keep an eye on cases involving old comrades and old enemies for the Sûreté. You can be sure that's enough to keep me busy."

He opened the folder and studied a document for a moment before he spoke again in a reflective tone. "You realize that power was lying on the ground during the war, and types like Paul Desmarais stooped to pick it up. Afterward, some of them found it hard to return to the plow like Cincinnatus."

"Life is different now."

"Yes, and some, even some of the brave and good, have found peace difficult."

"Victor Renard developed a taste for gambling."

"Which he was probably funding by blackmail. We have heard

rumors that he was putting pressure on his former associates, threatening to expose them as wartime profiteers. Your description of the notebook supports this theory."

"But wouldn't he have been vulnerable to exposure as well?" Pierre asked.

"Certainly. But he was without position and hence without shame. Plus the money he made could be put into a numbered Swiss account, beyond the reach of authorities here or in the United Kingdom."

"That doesn't explain why you are so sure that he was living as Victor Renard," I said.

"But this does." He ruffled through the folder and extracted a newspaper clipping with the very image of the late Madame Renard that had signaled the start of my troubles. Had she been the queen of spades she could not have been more ill-omened.

"The police claim not to know her real identity."

"They may claim that. To some extent, they may even be telling the truth—but not entirely. I know better. You said that you did not see her?"

"Just in the news photo."

"But I did," said Pierre. "I train out that way and I admired her car one day."

"Describe her for me, carefully."

"She was tall, rather broad shouldered, but thin. As if she was not in the best of health. Very pleasant, maybe a little lonely."

"And her voice?"

Pierre thought for a moment. "We exchanged only a few words, but low. She had a low, slightly hoarse voice. Too many cigarettes."

"I knew her," Hector said, "when her name was Gustave Gravois. A very close friend of Paul's. His little secret, one might say. Gravois was a fine amateur cyclist, who rode for your club,

Pierre, long before your time. But his real love was the cabaret stage. He performed an amusing act in drag, and he had a genuinely beautiful singing voice. He made a small fortune during the war entertaining the Germans in both his male and female personas."

Pierre made a face. "*Le cochon.*"

"Right, so after the war, when he was faced with difficulties, Gravois disappeared. He had a certain amount of money then, and if we are right about the blackmail scheme, he made more afterward as the contact person in France. He funneled Paul's threats and collected the cash."

"And hid in plain sight as Madame Renard?"

"That's right. The name was a little in-joke that had the advantage of shifting suspicion to the Chavanel ladies, who'd used 'Victor Renard' as a code for their business." He tapped the photo and took a long look at it. "As you see, the war aged him, and he was no longer welcome as a performer. Or perhaps he made himself up to look older. He was very skillful."

"Yet the police have given no hint of this!"

"It is common to retain a key piece of information, and while the gendarmes can hardly have missed his gender, they may still not know his real identity."

"Paul trusted him?" Pierre sounded dubious. "We assumed that he would have sent anything of value to his sister. Particularly if he was dying."

"His dying, like his death, may have been announced prematurely. But as for his sister, that's another story. We—and I mean both the Maquis and the Sûreté—were pretty sure that he had her husband murdered. She maybe didn't love her husband, but she loved being Madame Lambert. The two fell out."

"Now she's after his money in a serious way."

"Too serious. We will have to notify the authorities about the body in her villa. I can do that."

"Don't involve Inspector Chardin," I warned.

"No, not him. There are questions about him as well."

"There certainly are. He'd like to pin Madame Renard's killing on me, and he has retained my passport."

"Your passport will take some time to retrieve. In the meantime, it would be useful to learn more about why Madame Renard was murdered just at that time."

Oh-oh. I didn't like the sound of that. Hector might be an old comrade on the side of the angels, but he was still a copper, and he seemed to share the fraternity's desire to enlist my services. Well, if it would me keep out of his clutches, I could give him a theory gratis: "When Victor was shot, old pal László must have seen a chance to take over the racket and secure whatever they had already made. But he didn't know enough."

"László was never as smart as he thought," Hector agreed.

"Perhaps he figured that having me deliver the package would enable him to follow Madame Renard or to obtain the cipher key from her."

"He may not have known the name of the bank, either," Hector suggested.

"That is the last piece of the puzzle."

Hector smiled. "So the ladies were otherwise successful. That is very good. But our criminal case, as you can see, is all supposition. We have no proof of anything, and blackmail victims are unlikely to come forward once they are out of danger. We need to find where Madame Renard's effects are, which probably means uncovering another identity, possibly male."

"Or female. Or younger. Or older." A certain flexibility in such matters is ordinarily fine with me, but I could see complications multiplying exponentially and yours truly delayed ad infinitum. "If the police with their resources haven't found anything—"

"The police are not as interested as we are. They would have been happy to blame you for the killing. And would have, I'm sure, had you not delayed in delivering the package so long. It is one thing to retain information. It is quite another to fudge a time-of-death report by several days."

Procrastination equals salvation; I must remember that for the future. "Are we looking for the bank?" I asked.

"We are looking for a murderer. Or more precisely to catch a murderer, as I think we all agree that Serge Brun is involved in some way."

Oh, yes, we agreed about that.

"The bank is incidental to me," Hector concluded.

"But maybe not to the Chavanels."

"They would see the money went to good use," he said.

"And Cybèle?"

"It is for her, of course," Hector said quickly. "She sacrificed her youth to save our network. We are all in her debt."

I would like to have known how Romeo and Juliet saved Hector and the Chavanels, but he was disinclined to say anything more. Instead, he got down to our many practical problems, beginning with concealing the Renault, which was to be driven to a garage on the road back to town, where as Hector delicately put it, it would be "restored."

Next up would be a trip to a doctor for Pierre's broken ribs and then arrangements for a safe place for Pierre and me. That sounded good. What did not sound so appetizing was searching out the tracks of the late Gravois, aka Madame Renard. Of course, I said no a dozen times over, before twenty-four hours confined in a flat in Hector's oh-so-boring hamlet, watched over by an oh-so-boring ex-copper who proved both plain and straight, changed my mind.

A day later, still stiff and sore after my encounter with Brun and his associates, I was on the train for Nice wearing a borrowed black leather jacket and a pair of Hector's slacks, too short in the leg. I had money in my wallet, and my brief was to eat and drink and make new friends. I thought I could do that—if someone didn't kill me first.

CHAPTER SIXTEEN

Ah, azure sky and Homer's wine-dark sea—rather an exaggeration that, though the water was purple, definitely purple in the shadows under the rocks—with a handful of swimmers on every little white sand *plage*, and sunbathers draping themselves over the black rocks along the shore. If I remained on the Riviera, would my subject matter evolve? Would I begin to see gods and goddesses, water nymphs and Poseidon's train? I think not, though on closer examination, the Greek myths lose their prettiness, and the nymphs wind up in the ancient version of the fish locker, so maybe.

I was hoping that I wouldn't be on the Riviera long enough to know. It turns out that I really need London to paint. I need fog and rain and louche clubs drowned in smoke. I need nights gambling

JANICE LAW

with Arnold. I need Millais's old studio with Nan puttering about in the kitchen and endangering us by overlooking the gas. I really do. Instead, I was off looking for a ghost, who shifted between male and female and whose effects might be anywhere—or nowhere. I thought the latter most likely.

Hector had come to visit me in the "safe house," which was a second-story room above the local *tabac*, a room, Hector assured me, that had a history of sheltering brave men and women.

"I am a comedown for the residence," I said. "I am quite uninterested in being a hero."

"Never deal with anyone who *wants* to be a hero," Hector said. "They are dangerous for everyone concerned."

He was, like Shakespeare's Viola, fortified against all denials, and he'd come to brief me for my mission. He began with Brun, who ran a series of clubs in both Nice and Cannes. "I don't know if he actually owns them outright or if he provides expensive 'protection' for them, but either way, he controls them."

"With an associate called Richard Malet."

I got a sharp, quizzical look. "Someone you know?"

"I met him in passing. I think he'd promised Cybèle engagements at a better type of club."

Hector looked sad. "Cybèle is another person who has found the transition to peace difficult."

"Malet is out of the picture. I can assure you that he, too, has gone to ground."

Hector absorbed this for a moment. His almost immobile features transmitted amazingly delicate shades of feeling. "I see I did not make a mistake with you, Monsieur Lepage."

"Don't think it; everything was improvisation."

"Exactly what I meant. Now, here is what we know about Gustave Gravois/Madame Renard." He took out several photographs, square head shots that might once have graced identity cards—or wanted posters—and several old handbills with lettering in both French and German showing a very glamorous drag performer.

"He was good," I said.

"He had a kind of genius, and the strange thing was, though he didn't seem to be terribly interested in sex, his inclinations were more toward women than men."

"Yet you said Paul—"

"Paul was very much taken with him, and he was fond of Paul. What I'm trying to say is that there wasn't much passion in Gustave. Not of the everyday kind anyway. He came alive onstage and particularly in drag. When he was made up and performing, then he was lively and sexy. When he came out of the theater in his slacks and jacket, he was a good-looking man with some big thing missing inside." Hector looked thoughtful. "It was as if he'd left his soul in the dressing room."

I looked again at the newspaper clip announcing Madame Renard's death. When I'd first seen it, standing in the sun in Monaco, I'd thought that she had the face of a tragic heroine. In contrast, the mug shots of Gustave Gravois were totally forgettable. "In some cultures, men take all the women's parts in drama."

"Our sex is greedy for sensation," Hector remarked. "But for whatever reason, he was a different person onstage, and I think that's what Paul loved and could never reach, because the minute Gustave left the footlights he was ordinary and disinterested."

"The unattainable has a certain fascination."

"Exactly. Others came and went—women, boys—but Gustave retained his appeal long after he lost his looks. I think he must have gotten some little postwar engagements, not in the big halls and fancy clubs but somewhere, because performing was the breath of life for him."

I remembered the drag performer, the vocal equivalent of the beach caricaturist, who'd sung "The Man I Love." Surely there would be a place for an artiste who could actually sing. "You think that's how Brun found him? He heard him, recognized him, followed him?"

"Yes, and there's more. You described the shooting in London. Brun might have arranged that, too."

"With László's connivance?"

Hector shrugged. "It is possible."

"Brun will be on the lookout for me. And for Pierre."

"The reason I didn't want to involve him further. We want some evidence the police cannot ignore, and we want it quickly before the bicycle races when he will be out and vulnerable."

I had to agree with that; at the same time, one does not care to be expendable. "I feel a little like the big game hunter's goat."

Hector nodded. "Naturally, there is some risk in trying to flush Brun out, but you will be under a certain amount of surveillance— from old comrades and some sympathetic officers."

I didn't like the sound of that and said so, but Hector shook his head. "Too dangerous otherwise. Especially if you have been asking questions there already. Though this should help." He reached into his pocket and produced another identity card. This one was dirty and a bit smudged. "Not up to the Chavanels' standard, I'm afraid. But it will do."

I took a look at the image. He was my facial type, whoever he was, and at a quick glance the card might pass. "My hair isn't blond," I said, and though I hate to sound fussy, I added, "I really prefer darker for evening."

"It can be made blond." Hector opened up the kit bag he'd brought and produced a bottle of peroxide, an apron, a cape, rubber gloves, and some packets of yellow-brown hair dye. Monsieur

Hector of the Ritz! Would that a man of his ingenuity had stuck with the Sûreté. "You just need to look that little bit different," he said. "And Eugène Laroche is a nice name."

Great—I'd just about accustomed myself to Marcel, as in Proust, and now must think of myself as Eugène, as in Eugène of Savoy, military man extraordinaire, another fellow queer and genius. With a knowledgeable air, Hector put on the apron and gloves, draped me in the cape, and set to work quickly and neatly. "We strip the color out first, then dye it a dark blond."

I could feel my identity running off in interesting directions. It took Hector several hours, strong chemicals, and some work with the scissors, but eventually I emerged looking blond and vaguely German. "You were an admirer of Gustave's when he was entertaining during the war," Hector said. "His stage name was Mademoiselle Veronique."

"I can imagine that. What was I doing here?"

"Do you speak a little German by any chance?"

"I speak a lot of German, most of it naughty."

"That will do very nicely. You'll an be Alsatian black marketer."

"I know nothing about either."

Hector tried again. "You are British but were stranded by the war in France. You fell in with black marketers."

I could see tedious reminiscences about stock pricing and smuggling and the running of heavy trucks. "What about I was stranded by the war in France and was kept in chocolates and Champagne by a rich German officer?"

Hector laughed. "Very well. Invent a name for him."

"Not on your life! I'm the soul of discretion as a 'gentleman's gentleman.' But he'd be—what should he be? I rather fancy an *Oberstleutnant* in the Wehrmacht."

"I'm surprised you didn't go all the way to general."

"Too much about a general might be remembered; besides, my real love is the 'other ranks.'"

"No chocolates and Champagne there." Hector held up the identity card and the hand mirror. No one who knew me would be fooled, but I figured I would pass a casual inspection. "Very reasonable."

Hector took off the cape and his apron and gloves. He sat down next to me to go over a list of clubs that might have employed Gravois. "You're looking for friends, contacts. You've been away. You hadn't heard of his disappearance."

"Some will surely know he's dead."

"It will be a very great shock to you when you learn," Hector suggested.

"If I find his flat, his house wherever he was living? Is breaking and entering on the menu?"

"We can take care of that," Hector said quickly. He gave me a number. "The *tabac*. Leon will always give me a message promptly."

Why do I get involved in these half-assed schemes? I wondered, and maybe Hector was thinking along the same lines, because there was a long pause. "You're sure Brun will be around?" I asked. "You don't think he's off to Switzerland with Yvette Lambert?"

"According to what you've told us, he still doesn't know which bank and he doesn't have the account number."

"Unless Yvette knew."

"That she was still in France two nights ago suggests she does not have all the information, either."

"She was planning to disappear, though. She intended the dead woman to be mistaken—even temporarily—for herself."

"Yes, and that worried me. But you and Pierre recovered what we think was the key, the parts catalog. The Chavanels and Joubert have copies of the notebook, and the letter has been lost."

"Or is in her possession—or Brun's." Though the Chavanels

were closest to the jackpot, I admitted reluctantly that no one had all the information.

"However much money Brun could potentially get, he can't let go of the clubs until he has that information," Hector said.

That made sense if anything did, but was Brun sensible? "Was he always a killer?"

Hector shrugged. "Before the war he was a low-level thug. The war brought out the worst in him, and sad to say the Resistance gave him skills that he's turned to bad use. Though I understand now that he doesn't like to get his hands dirty, that he contracts everything out."

"To the likes of Richard Malet?"

Hector nodded.

"There's someone else I want to know about, Jerome Chavanel. He was a cousin of the old ladies and a waiter at the Hotel Negresco, who was murdered at the end of the war, stabbed in the back, the same MO that almost finished me. If I have the chronology accurate, that happened soon after Cybèle arrived in Nice. I was told that he had good contacts in the clubs and theaters. I want to know if there's a connection."

After a long enough pause to make me uneasy, Hector said, "Everyone rich and powerful went to the Negresco. Jerome was in position to learn a great deal, and he frequently passed on useful information to the Resistance."

"On the side of the angels then."

"Well, most of the time. There was also an unproven suspicion that he was a contact for either the Gestapo or for the Abwehr."

"Cybèle arrived just before his murder. Bad timing, maybe, given her reputation?"

"I'm afraid so. The poor child was not to know and, being innocent, never dreamed." He shook his head as if shaking off bad thoughts, worse memories. "We were all to blame, but with the war winding down, we hoped to resume ordinary lives once more."

"I was under that illusion and look where it's gotten me."

"Exactly."

"Yet a German private, barely more than a boy—how could that have suggested anything more than folly and impulse?"

"Is that what she told you?"

"The old ladies. Cybèle denied everything."

"And quite rightly. Her lover—if I can use the term though I'd rather not—was fairly high up in the Gestapo, a *Kriminalinspektor*. She got picked up on some minor infraction, dodgy coupons, I think, though I suspect they already had their eyes on the family. When she was brought in, he spotted her, dismissed the charges out of hand, squired her home, and discovered Agathe's cooking. He probably had enough to arrest them all, and if he had, he'd have rolled up our network." When I looked surprised, he added, "We assumed that no one held out for more than twenty-four hours; the working assumption was that we'd be betrayed. That was wisest."

"But the *Kriminalinspektor* had other ideas?"

"He was no fanatic. The war was going badly and his career was shot, so he figured to enjoy himself while everything went to hell. He was willing to work a deal: the favors of Mademoiselle and dinners at the Chavanels' residence in exchange for a blind eye. Of course, it was not put so bluntly. It was a hint here or there." He lifted his shoulders. "You will think badly of us. She was just sixteen and very brave."

"And no one knew the real situation?"

"Some knew and sought to take advantage later, like Paul Desmarais. That was when he was working with the Americans, swaggering around with a Browning automatic and a jeep at his disposal. He went in a big way for denunciations, for rooting out

Fascist elements and straying women. Really, he was settling old scores and eliminating old rivals."

I began to see Cybèle's contacts with Brun and his circle in a different light.

"Yet hadn't he worked with the Chavanels earlier?"

"Indeed, until they figured out that he was stripping their clients of pretty much all their assets. The ladies can be tough, and Anastasie is idealistic. Paul didn't like being called to account—even as mildly as they could afford to do it. I think they had something on him, too. I think they did, because he never moved directly against them, only against Cybèle, and only when the Milice was history and he was working for the Yanks and looking for the exit door."

A piece of work. I must remember that and also that he might not be dead. Be on the lookout, Eugène, I thought, as we rumbled into Nice. *Be alert*, as we used to say in the ARP, and keep your eyes open for ghosts and ghouls and the very much alive Serge Brun, who must by now have figured out that at least one of his colleagues was not coming back. Whether or not I had any luck tracing the friends of the late Gustave Gravois, I was sure that my visit to the old belle epoque burg would be filled with incident.

CHAPTER SEVENTEEN

Have I mentioned my fondness for sailors? I have a weakness, as
Nan would say, for members of the maritime profession, for the
toilers of the sea, for jolly jack-tars and also the not-so-jolly ones,
who are really more to my taste. But Nice, alas, is not a naval port:
no smart white-and-blue uniforms, no gay striped shirts and red
pom-pom-topped caps. Nice had hard-eyed fishermen and workers on the cement boats and the ferry trade, few promising enough
to make the port-side bistros appealing. But eventually full dark
descended, the nightclubs, smart or seedy, got in full swing, and
café society came out to play.

I wandered along a brightly lit street, searching out Hector's
likely prospects, Le Chien Rouge, Le Nouveau Mayfair, La Voile

Noire, Bacchus, and El Grec. I'd decided that Eugène was a gay dog, and at each one, I had a few drinks, listened to the headliner, and flirted with other patrons. I was in full bon vivant mode and after applauding a singer who squawked through "As Time Goes By," or "L'amour est un jeu," it was easy to say, "Know who I miss? Mademoiselle Veronique. Anyone remember her?" And sometimes to add, "Gustave. That was his name. Gustave G-something, Gravois, I think. Yes, Gustave Gravois, but he usually performed as Mademoiselle Veronique. Now there was a voice."

Reaction to this gambit varied. Incomprehension, mostly; the war was ever present and under the rug simultaneously, while prewar seemed as ancient as Babylonia, and the only allowable nostalgia was a few old songs. Most claimed never to have heard Gravois, though a chap who knew the mademoiselle had "sung for the Krauts" punched me a good one, with the result that we both landed on the sidewalk. I hoped that he'd prove interesting in one way or another, but he was just a drunk with a temper. With dwindling possibilities of success and needing a restorative drink, I tried a little ramshackle place with a garden seating area. The headliner last seen on the memorable night when I entered the gravediggers' fraternity had squeezed himself into a tight red satin gown to warble "Un amour comme le nôtre." I took a seat at one of the tables, ordered Champagne, and sent my compliments to the chanteuse, who sashayed over at the end of his set, his makeup softening in the heat.

"Champagne! For me? My dear, this is a special night. One's work is so seldom appreciated."

I could certainly believe that—but I have a tin ear for music. "Your singing takes me back to café life before the war."

"Before my time," he said kittenishly. "Professionally speaking."

He embroidered a bit on his extreme youth, though he was forty if he was a day. He was quite amusing, but I'm not so fond of campy acquaintances. I really prefer straight men, pun intended, because I like to camp it up myself and have the best lines. Still, this was work, this was business, this was dedication. I listened in silence, bought him some chocolates to go with the bubbly, and worked the conversation round to my prewar favorite, Mademoiselle Veronique. "Such a talent, such a voice. One could forget everything listening to Mademoiselle Veronique."

I thought that the name made him uneasy, but he asked about her repertoire. Repertoire! Hector hadn't briefed me that thoroughly. "Rather like yours," I said. "And lieder, of course." I seemed to remember that the Berlin of my misspent youth had been fond of lieder.

"Lieder is for artists, but I expect she had a hard time. There was not much call for lieder here during the war."

"In certain quarters it remained popular."

"I wouldn't know about those." He drew himself up in a way that rather spoiled the illusion of his décolletage. "Monsieur, I am a patriot."

I raised my glass. "I wouldn't have dreamed otherwise. But Mademoiselle Veronique lived for the stage. One might even say she only lived onstage. Her choices would not be our choices, yours and mine, I mean, but consider that irreplaceable voice! So I've been looking out for her. She might do well to consider leaving France, having a flutter elsewhere."

He poured himself another glass and shook his head. "Alas, Monsieur, the name doesn't sound familiar."

"The name, what's in a name? 'The rose by any other name would smell as sweet,' etc. etc." I took out one of the handbills and laid it on the table.

"Oh, Hotel Negresco. Very nice. Lovely acoustics, décor to die for. And that dress! Not the thing now, of course, except in clubs catering to a certain age. Old-fashioned, you know. But splendid," he admitted, "splendid." He ran his finger down the line of the tea gown, which was softly draped, semisheer, and lavishly embroidered.

"Everything about Mademoiselle Veronique was first class," I said. "And what was surprising was that Gustave himself was unprepossessing." I slid one of the photos of Gustave Gravois across the table. This time there was no doubt: He recognized the face.

"Oh," he said. "I hadn't realized."

"You do know him, then?"

"Oh, yes, though not personally. He's been singing and introducing the headliners in clubs for half a year. Le Chien Rouge. He was in Le Chien Rouge—when? Let's see. I find time flies, dear, especially on the wings of Champagne." There was an edge of bitterness in his voice. "Must be a month ago now." He looked again at the handbill and compared it to Gravois's image. "I'd never have guessed he was such a queen. Though you are right, a good voice, still expressive if worn at the edges. Too good really for the work he's doing, but he shows no spark, none of the true artistic fire."

He seemed set to go on in this vein, and I said, "Art was for Mademoiselle Veronique."

"Must have been. Remarkable!"

"You said about a month ago for his engagement at Le Chien Rouge. Have you seen him since?"

"My own engagements have kept me occupied, but no, I haven't seen him around lately."

"A pity. I am only in Nice briefly. Who might know how to reach him?"

"Le Chien Rouge is one of Serge Brun's clubs. You might track him down." When he smiled, he showed a pair of long canines. "But no one asks Serge too many questions, if you get my meaning."

I did indeed. "Anyone else who might know where he lives?"

"I do," he said unexpectedly. "I know because he rented a room in the same apartment as a friend of mine, a young dancer I know. Nice girl. You find her, you'll find out about him, too, though I haven't seen her lately, either. She used to stop by after her shows. I'd walk her home and she'd do alterations for me."

I held my breath, for I sensed what was coming.

"I don't know her real name; we performers live in our own theatrical world, you know, dear, but Mademoiselle Justine is her stage name. She lives just north of the port." He gave me the address.

I thanked him profusely and got up.

"You're not leaving when there's still Champagne!"

I took his hand and kissed it. "For you," I said and made my escape. Cybèle had been living in the same apartment building as Gustave Gravois, aka Mademoiselle Veronique, aka Madame Renard. Even the insouciant Eugène needed time to think that over, and at two a.m. after a trawl through the cafés of Nice, neither he nor I was feeling too sharp. According to plan, my duties were ended; I could phone the *tabac* and pass on the message to Hector. But not at this hour. This was the hour for good burghers and even ex-Sûreté men to be in their beds, and for night birds like yours truly to walk off the evening's indulgences. I headed north.

The streets were quiet. I like that. I like darkness and long shadows and the moon behind clouds, all of which take me back to the blackout and bombers' moons and the threat of imminent destruction from the air. Horrid at the moment, but curiously stimulating in retrospect, teasing the mind with images and fragments that I must learn how to render. I walked the night streets of Nice with images of strange rooms and strange bodies roiling against luminous gray, pink, and orange backgrounds; I would experiment with those as soon as I got back to London where I could paint.

The apartment building was on a shady street lined with plane trees. There were mopeds chained to the iron railings, and a welter of garbage cans to one side. The old building had come down in the world, but it was classic French architecture with long windows, decorative stucco work, and balconies running the length of the façade and swooping along the sides. I wondered if there would still be a prying, sleepless concierge on the premises. Eugène thought so, but I recalled the irregular hours and careless arrangements of the theatrical profession and decided to try the front door. I wasn't surprised to discover that the building was unlocked.

Inside there was just enough light to make out the names on the mailboxes: several married couples and, on the fourth floor, *P. Moreau, Musician*, who must give lessons at home. The other labels gave no clue to either sex or occupation: *O. Blanchard, R. Lefevre, P. Roche, V. Garnier*—and *C. Chavanel* in 32. Cybèle, third floor. But there was no G. Gravois and no sign of Madame Renard, either. Eliminating the couples and Cybèle left five possibilities. I leaned toward V. Garnier in 36, as the name combined the initial letters of Veronique and Gravois, but given Gravois's musical gifts it wasn't inconceivable that he had been instructor P. Moreau in 42, directly above Cybèle.

In any case, P. Moreau would be Eugène's entrée, for while music leaves me cold, he had developed a sudden desire for singing lessons. I was pondering the approach and trying to work up enthusiasm for the vocal art when I heard footsteps outside. A tardy resident or part of the "surveillance" Hector had mentioned? Ought Eugène to walk out like a solid citizen or beat a strategic retreat? Common sense said leave; the knife that had shattered my painting kit said hide. The lobby was bare and, except for whatever might be upstairs or down, offered not the slightest refuge. I decided on the stairs. I reached the first landing as the door opened and crouched behind the ornate iron railings supporting the banister.

Someone large in the lobby—the light was too dim to make out more than that he was wearing a dark suit and a wide-brimmed trilby that shaded his face. He inspected the mailboxes as I had done. Not a resident then, and I crept across the hall and up the second flight. I didn't think that he heard me, but he followed. I could see his shadow, elongated by the light below, wavering on the wall. It moved with a curious halting motion as if he were lame or too ill to take the stairs easily. That proved to be my good luck, for before he reached the second floor, I'd made the third. C. Chavanel's apartment was in the middle at the back and her door was securely locked. I hadn't time to try the others. At the end of the hall, one of the long windows gave out onto the balcony. I pushed it open and climbed out.

Three stories below were the alley and the spiky feathers of a palm tree. The balcony appeared to circle the building, each apartment's outdoor space delineated by a quarter circle of spiked metal. I didn't see much hope from the lighted front of the building, which was directly on the street. The back was probably darker and might give access to Cybèle's flat. I tested the metal barrier with a shake— a slight wobble but not too bad. Did I hear someone in the hall? The sound of an uneven footstep?

With that inspiration, I took a breath, seized one of the rusty decorative points, put my foot on another lower one, and swung out over the pavement below. The barrier shifted down a fraction, and I made a frantic grab for purchase on the other side with my left hand. Another shift, this time definitely downward. I straddled the points, risking a good deal of excitement and future happiness, then swung myself around, precipitating a shower of rust flakes and causing the ironwork to screech but enabling me to put one foot on the neighboring balustrade. Despite a number of scratches, I was able to step down onto the floor of the balcony. Terra firma. I maneuvered around a potted plant and took shelter behind the awning that was hanging loosely from its framework. Then I waited.

The moon flirted with the clouds, lightening and darkening the façade, but there was no sound from either the apartment behind me or the hallway. Perhaps I had risked a drop of three stories for no good reason. Perhaps I could maneuver my way back, walk down the hall, and find my way out. Perhaps, but I was loath to risk that particular piece of ironwork again. Onward, Eugène! I banged my shins on a little metal table, caught a chair just before it went over, and reached the next barrier, this one right at the rear corner of the building. Another little adventure with gravity and aging metal. During the war, I got over any fear of heights fire watching in church steeples with Arnold. I hadn't imagined that being up forty, fifty feet and higher with the imminent threat of high explosives would ever pay dividends.

The first apartment was occupied by gardeners who owned a small grove of plants, scented and laden with pollen. I stifled what had promised to be a titanic sneeze and picked my way cautiously around pots and saucers, watering cans, and miniature garden implements. Behind the greenery, the apartment shutters were closed and locked, and somewhere within, my eternal nemesis, a small dog, began to bark. I swung out on the barrier without waiting to test it. With a nasty creak, it dropped me a good four inches toward oblivion, before I got a foot on the ledge of the balustrade. The whole construction seemed set to pull away from the masonry. I threw my weight against the spikes—uncomfortable business—and bracing myself against the balustrade, swung around the barrier, which listed alarmingly to deposit me on what I hoped was Cybèle's share of the balcony. I forced the barrier back as far as it would go and got into the shadows behind an open shutter on the French doors.

A man's voice next door began arguing with the dog, which with the mad persistence of its species, continued to insist on alarms and strangers and problems on the balcony. I heard French doors creak open and stopped breathing. The dog rattled the pots on its way to the barrier, where it planted itself and began a row that ended only when the exasperated owner carried it back inside. The whole canine tribe has it in for me.

I sat down on the floor of the balcony and waited until I was pretty sure that no one was afoot. Then I examined Cybèle's apartment. While the shutters had been left half open, the French doors were locked. The first window I tried was secured, but though the other one had both shutters closed, they were not hooked and the window behind was wide open: Cybèle was a wonderful girl. I maneuvered over the sill into a once spacious room broken up into a bedroom and a jutting cubicle that proved to be a WC/bath combination. The bed was empty, the bathroom likewise. I moved through the kitchenette and the living room, closed the shutters, and checked that the main door was locked before turning on a light.

Some shabby furniture, some good dresses, and piles of sheet music that suggested Cybèle was conscientious. I approved; performers should work hard as should painters. Some dishes drying in a rack. She was tidy and had expected to be back after her evening performance. I saw that she was thrifty and ate some of her meals at home, because I found the end of a baguette, a bit of cheese, and a melon. A few phone numbers were scribbled on a pad. One was "Serge" and I guessed that was Serge Brun. No surprise; she had worked for him. Her purse was with her, so no money in the flat and no passport, though I found her bankbook. Either she was doing rather well at the clubs or Serge had paid her lavishly to impersonate Madame Renard.

That was the sum total of my discoveries; I had risked my neck for nothing. I wandered back to the kitchen and squeezed the baguette experimentally. It was going stale but it wasn't rock hard as it should be after several days on the kitchen counter. I got a knife and opened the melon and found it delicious. Even the cheese was edible, and that fact, combined with the missing passport, made me wonder if Cybèle had come back to the apartment. Would she carry a passport to work? I didn't think so, though perhaps she feared she'd have to make a quick exit. But either way, she'd been back for some reason. I was sure of it.

I turned off the light. All was quiet. I could leave and make my report tomorrow, but at near two a.m., I'd still have to find a hotel or sleep in the *gare*. I decided that my encounters with rickety balconies and hysterical dogs deserved some reward. I went through to Cybèle's bedroom and flopped down on the spread, which smelled of face powder and her flowery perfume, echoes of a life through the looking glass. Was that what Gravois had liked? Had Mademoiselle Veronique been the door to an alternate life for him, a life with fabulous clothes and a first-rate talent and a gangster lover? I tried to imagine what that would be like, and I felt an irrational desire to see his apartment. In the morning, I told myself, and within minutes I was sound asleep.

Sparrows in the trees, a moped puttering off, a car door slamming, thin silver bars between the shutters. Was that what woke me? I registered the fuchsia silk spread, a maroon light shade, pale lavender walls, a ceiling too high and ornate to belong to the truncated room below: Cybèle's flat. Early. And then I heard it again, the sound that, out of all the urban noise, had awakened me. Someone was moving about in the flat above: number 42, residence of P. Moreau, music teacher. Whoever it was had a heavy, uneven, and rather slow tread like the man who had come in behind me last night. Perhaps he really was Monsieur Moreau, up and ready for a day of scales and squalling. Or perhaps, like me, he wanted access to Gravois's old apartment. Eugène would soon find out.

I got out of bed, used the en suite, and stepped into the hall.

All quiet. Outside, shopkeepers were opening their metal grills and hosing off the sidewalks. I stopped at the first *tabac* for a coffee and the phone. I called the number Hector had given me and left the message that Eugène would attempt a music lesson from P. Moreau, flat 42, and repeated the address twice. The keeper of the zinc promised to give Hector the information.

I hung up and went in search of a *boulangerie*, bought croissants, and loitered under the plane trees to keep an eye on the apartment building. I told myself that I was just going to await the appearance of the man with the limp. That I would see if he was my "Victor Renard" from London. That all I wanted was a complete report for Hector. That I was going to be sensible.

Two women left with baskets and string bags for some early shopping. A dark sedan passed twice, but the man with the limp did not appear. Neither did Hector's promised "surveillance" or any curious gendarmes. Prudence said, wait, but Eugène was in an antic mood. People who know me would mostly say that I need sex and drink and fooling about to live. All true, but what I need to keep on anything like an even keel is painting, an unending fascination that sops up excess energy and channels the imagination onto canvas. Without it, I'm inclined to take risks and get up to capers like imagining myself Eugène Laroche, who, at precisely eight o'clock, walked up the four flights to P. Moreau's flat and knocked on the door.

I was confident that I would know at once if this were the right apartment, if this was where Gravois had transformed himself and entered other worlds. I liked the idea, but there was no response. Had he left in the few minutes while I phoned from the *tabac*? I knocked again and waited. Then I recognized the step that had awakened me earlier. The door opened a few inches.

"Monsieur Moreau?"

There was the briefest hesitation, but it told me that whoever he was, he was not Moreau. "What do you want?"

"Eugène Laroche. I've heard you're a marvelous teacher. I was talking with someone just last night, singer I heard, really quite good, and I was saying how I wished I could sing and he said, try Monsieur Moreau. And gave me your address."

The door opened a little more—was my assumption wrong? Was I about to have to pay for an actual lesson in the fine art of caterwauling?

"It's barely eight a.m."

Even though the shutters were half closed and his face was against the morning light, he had the same black hair, same lean face, same malevolent black eyes. I recognized Victor Renard, last seen with his life's blood pouring out of him, Victor Renard, who was almost certainly a long time lowlife named Paul Desmarais, back from the nearly dead.

"Commercial traveler. Art supplies, don't you know. Linseed oil, damar varnish, hand-ground colors from all the best manufacturers. Here today, Marseille tomorrow, up in Montpellier the day after. Time and tide and the SNCF wait for no man. I thought I could meet you and set up a lesson for, say, next week?"

I half expected that he would slam the door in my face and that would have been quite all right with me; I wasn't sure I fancied any closer contact with him.

"Come in," he said and opened the door wide.

The flat had taken some damage—I saw cracked glass on some pictures, slashed upholstered furniture, a broken vase, drawers pulled out. Could that have been Cybèle's work? Could she have tried the same balcony route I'd used and turned over the flat in quest for bank documents? It was a thought. I guessed that Paul had spent the night tidying up, for though the bookcases were empty, their contents were now in neat piles on the floor, and there was a brush and shovel and a large wastebasket full of debris. I thought a trifle better of him for that. But only a trifle.

"I see you are redecorating. I can come back next week without any trouble."

He went over to the piano, a white baby grand, surely the instrument of Mademoiselle Veronique, who looked down from a large and handsomely framed poster reminiscent of the handbill Hector had given me. It had survived the search untouched. "You've never sung?" Paul asked.

"No, no, this is just a whim, old chap. But under the influence of wine and song, I thought, 'Have a go, Eugène.'" I hoped I wouldn't have to be Eugène too long. I found his taste for jolly slang irritating.

To my surprise, Paul sat down at the piano and played a snatch of something. I smiled as if I recognized the damn thing and said, "very nice." I got a vicious look in return, and I guessed that it was one of Mademoiselle Veronique's songs.

"Scales," he said. "Scales are the foundation. Key of C." He began hitting one key after another. Now you."

"Ahhh."

"Not 'ah,' 'do.' Do, re, mi. Like this." And he demonstrated. His voice sounded no worse than my informant of last night. Presumably he'd picked up some tips from Gravois, if not the Mademoiselle. Then he hit C again and waited until I found the note.

"*Bien.* We have C! Seven notes to go." He gave me another "I could eat your liver" look. He did not have what I'd say was a gift for pedagogy, but then he didn't have much of a pupil. "Next note."

I began to wish that I'd paid even minimal attention to music instruction at school. "Do, re . . ." I sounded like a donkey and felt like one too.

"Mi, mi, mi, mi." He pounded the key emphatically, but I

couldn't help noticing that he seemed to be listening for more than my desperate attempts to match the noises from the piano. A life of vigilance? Or something more?

I found "mi" and we struggled all the way to "do" again. The damn thing repeated: the horrors of math combined with noise! "Perhaps enough for today," I suggested. "Your fee?"

He leaned back on the piano bench and looked at me closely. "I'm not sure you are suitable for a pupil," he said. He reached into the instrument and pulled out a revolver.

"I hadn't realized music was such a demanding profession," I said. "I'm rethinking torch songs and lieder."

Paul did not have a sense of humor, and I would have faced severe difficulties if someone hadn't knocked on the door. My spirits rose. My surveillance? A handsome squad of gendarmes? Too soon, I thought.

"Sing," Paul commanded, and he hit the keys noisily.

My dry throat did not improve my performance.

"Again!"

Back to do, re, mi. The third time through, Paul rose from the piano. He put my hands on the keys and motioned with the revolver for my singing to continue. Great. Struggling vocally, I'd been launched into instrumental music. What were the black keys? Stick to white. ". . . fa, so, la . . ." What came next? Do? No, ti. "Ti, do."

He waved the revolver again and moved softly to the door. As I searched for C, I gauged the quickest way to get myself safely behind the piano. Paul checked the spy hole, flipped the lock, and, keeping himself back against the wall, jerked the door open. Serge Brun stood in the doorway. When I dived off the bench, he fired at the movement. The shot echoed around the room, followed by two, three more. I scuttled back from the piano to the shelter of a substantial bureau. Paul shouted and I looked up. Through a cloud of smoke, I saw Brun twitching on the floor, and Paul standing impassively with the revolver in his hand.

"We leave now," he said.

CHAPTER EIGHTEEN

I stood up, still half protected by the bureau. Serge Brun had stopped flopping like a landed fish, and my semiexpert diagnosis was that he was beyond anything this ex-ARP warden could offer. I took that as an excuse to stay where I was, with no need to be officious and perhaps jog Paul's memory of another good Samaritan.

He jerked his head and swung his revolver: time to move out. Involuntarily, I edged back toward the French doors. I definitely did not want to go anywhere with Paul Desmarais. He raised the weapon, and I froze, but either Eugène or I or both of us were beyond panic, because it came into my mind that Paul must need me for something. Otherwise, why hadn't he already fired?

Eugène began nattering about his sales route and difficult connections with the SNCF. Paul cut him off. "Go into the bedroom," he said.

Were outré adventures with sex and death in my future? I backed uneasily around the bureau and made my way to the rear of the apartment. It had acquired the same awkward mod-com as Cybèle's, but the décor was elegant and expensive, anchored by a fine brass four-poster with a ruffled canopy. A sign of Mademoiselle Veronique's taste, I was sure. The bed sported a paisley spread in a variety of purples, and sitting on top were two large leather suitcases bound up with straps.

"Hurry up." Paul gestured toward the cases. My function suddenly became clear: porter extraordinaire. I picked up the heavy luggage and staggered through to the living room. "Understand if you run, I will kill you."

I didn't feel able to debate this, though I could not help pausing as we passed the late Serge Brun.

"No blood, no blood," Paul warned. He opened the door and gestured down the hall. "Back stairs, quickly."

I thought I heard voices below; four shots could hardly have been ignored. The neighbors would be asking one another if that had really been a gun, and someone would hustle off to summon the police. I felt the barrel of the revolver in the small of my back and went along to the stairwell. Paul limped painfully behind me, but hampered by the big cases, I could not move fast enough to get beyond the range of his revolver, and I guessed that he would shoot immediately if I jettisoned the luggage. On the ground floor, I set down the cases. Paul waved his revolver. "One more," he said.

My adventures in the hinterlands had put me off basements, and I was set to balk when there was a commotion in the lobby. Had someone telephoned? Had police arrived already? I wondered if I could swing a case into Paul or drop one to distract him and raise the alarm. Most likely the result would be more shots, some aimed at me. I started down the stairs, which was steep and narrow, without any landing. At the bottom, Paul opened the door into the basement. I had bad images of darkness and death, but he forced me toward the faint glimmer of one of the light wells and opened the exterior door beside it. "Remember what I told you," he said.

We climbed out to an alley, my arms stretched to the ground with the weight of the cases, and reached the street that ran behind the apartment building. Paul seemed unconcerned by the shooting, nosy neighbors, and the imminent arrival of gendarmes. But, of course, he was not P. Moreau; he was unknown and so was I. We might be a couple of provincial visitors, perhaps father and son or uncle and nephew. He was ill or convalescent—notice his limp and the one hand in his pocket—and I was the dutiful assistant carrying all the luggage. Really, there was nothing to worry about. I told myself that and repeated it to Eugène.

We walked to the street corner. "Put down one case and flag a cab," he said, adding, "I shoot the driver, if you try anything."

I stepped to the curb and scanned the street both ways. Naturally when you want a cab, there are none. And when, as at that moment, you don't particularly want a cab—or can't decide whether escape or capture will be best—one appears. The driver made a dashing U-turn and pulled up beside us. He hopped out to open the trunk, but Paul insisted that we keep the luggage inside with us.

"Certainly, Monsieur," the driver said. He was short and stocky with a broad, dark face and the liquid black eyes so common in the south. His nose was aquiline, his mouth thin, his expression, skeptical. He looked like a man of experience, and I guessed some of it was dubious. He opened the rear door. Paul motioned me in and the cabbie piled the cases on top of me, then helped Paul, still with one hand in his pocket, into the cab. Paul gave him the address, and we pulled into the early morning traffic. As we rode, I considered various escape scenarios. Throw the cases onto Paul, shout a warning to the cabbie? I could barely move under the weight, and there was little room to maneuver in the small backseat.

Open the door? Throw a case out and follow it, tumbling onto the ground like a cowboy in the westerns Arnold enjoys? Cars and trucks passing and a landing on cement were all against that plan, and I tended to believe Paul when he threatened to shoot the driver; he seemed beyond fear—or maybe beyond hope. I occupied myself with possibilities, none good, until to my surprise, I heard Paul say, "Turn in here."

I'd expected another run to the mountains—or at least some quiet suburb; instead, we'd arrived at an area of warehouses and small works near the docks. I thought of the fish locker, and had I seen any sign of fins or delivery vans, I'd have opened the door and taken my chances.

The cab bounced over the rutted and potholed entranceway and came to a halt. "The cases," Paul said to me. He climbed out to pay the driver, which he managed one handed, the cabbie kindly helping him with his wallet, while all the time he had both of us within range of his weapon.

The cab drove away in a cloud of fine white dust, and we were left standing in front of a garage with a loading dock at the side. Paul motioned toward this building with his head; he rationed his words as if he were paying by the syllable. We climbed up the ramp, and he told me to put down the cases and lift one of the doors. Inside were a pickup truck and several vans. After a brief inspection, Paul selected a high, boxy olive-green van and had me open the passenger door. Then he took the revolver from his pocket. This is it, I thought, and I picked up a case, quick as I could, and held it in front of my body.

"Put it in the cab," he said, "and get in the back."

I didn't move. He lifted the weapon. "I'm a very good shot," he said.

He'd fired three times at Brun, but this didn't seem to be the right time to discuss marksmanship. I put the case on the passenger's seat and moved to the back of the vehicle. Space to run? Anywhere to hide? Good-sized rear windows lit the garage, but there was no back exit visible. Paul had guessed my thought, because he was right behind me. He gestured for me to open the back of the van, and when I'd climbed inside, he slammed the door shut and dropped the latch in place. I was in the body of the van, which had been closed off from the driver's compartment by a sturdy wood and metal barrier. The only light came from two dirty oval windows in the rear doors.

I heard Paul move around the van; he threw in the second case, closed the passenger door, opened the driver's, then started the vehicle. Where to now? I braced myself against the rear doors and watched the rutted parking lot meld into the busy city streets. I was safe enough in town, I decided, and as the van swayed and lurched, I stopped worrying about our route and began to examine the interior.

It was some sort of work van with a variety of odd holes and patches and a series of floor braces and brackets seemingly designed to trip up any unfortunate passenger. After my second tumble, I remembered Pierre's informative discussion of alternate wartime fuels. This machine had probably been fitted with a boiler or some big receptacle for burning wood or charcoal and now, with better times, had been restored to gasoline power. Unfortunately, the conversion seemed to have been carried out carefully; none of the closed-off openings were accessible and the whole business was depressingly sturdy.

There was a familiar smell, however. I recognized it nearly at once, and my newest alter ego, Eugène, did too, as well he might, because it combined turpentine, linseed oil, and paint of one sort or another. Holding on to the interior ribs of the van, I made my way toward the front. A few old paint rags, a mostly empty can of thinner. A pothole in the road threw me against the barrier dividing the driver's compartment from the body of the van.

As my eyes became accustomed to the dim light, I saw that the barrier had been fitted up with shelves to hold paints and supplies. Most were empty, but on the lowest shelf I found two gallon cans of paint—Paul's cursory examination had missed those. From their weight, I figured both were more than half full. I swung one experimentally and narrowly missed striking the side of the van. Though the can was heavy enough to do damage, I was sure that Paul was too cautious to let me approach with any potential weapon.

I shook first one can and then the other. Still liquid. I tried to lift the tops with my fingernails, but slops of old paint had sealed them up tight. After a frantic search for something to pry off the lids, I settled on a stray penny that I found in my trouser pocket. It bent and twisted, but I managed to pry off both lids. Leathery skins the color of rancid cream covered the paint. With a thick splinter from a floorboard as a stirrer, I punctured the paint surface and began to turn messes of white lead, one of my favorite pigments, into the resinous vehicle. Once I had the paint reconstituted and the pigment liquefied, I poured one can into the other, gave a final stir, and made my way—awkwardly and with slopping paint—to the rear of the van.

Paul would stop. He would open the rear door as he had before, gun in his right hand, left hand on the door. Saving his breath for something more precious, he would gesture with the gun. That would be the moment. Alternately, he might open the door, again with his left hand, and step back behind it. *Be alert for that, Francis!*

Then I would wait until he leaned in to threaten me. Yes, I thought either tack would do; I would just have to guess correctly. And hope we were alone, though if he had associates in crime, all was up anyway, for I was convinced that I was only alive because of his debility.

So, time to wait. I sat down by the door, the paint bucket to hand, and—as Nan likes to say—"possessed my soul in patience." The Mediterranean sun beat down on the metal roof and streamed in the rear windows. I deduced we were heading northwest, back toward the Var and the Villa Mimosa, Paul's territory where everything had started so long ago. I wondered if Hector's "surveillance," the reality of which I half doubted, had any idea what had happened and whether he had received my message.

As we rode farther and the van grew hotter, I grew less sanguine about my prospects. A trick with the paint can seemed increasingly feeble, and I began thinking of last messages, which brought me back to Paul Desmarais, who had written a message when he thought he was dying but hadn't died after all. There were still some very queer things about that and about Paul, who had been hit in the upper chest and nearly bled to death, but who had survived with a limp. Where had that come from?

I tried to remember the scene at the gambling club, at how the man in the blue overcoat had turned up his collar and hunched his shoulders, but I couldn't bring up a vision of his gait. I'd been fascinated by the gesture, by the way his back curved and his neck sank back into his shoulders; I hadn't picked up the way he moved his legs. Joking with Arnold, "flying on the wings of Champagne" like the chanteuse, I'd seen the man descending the stairs with one hand, I now remembered, on the banister.

Just that, nothing more. I closed my eyes, and I was trying to focus on black hair, a blue overcoat, long shadows from the lights of the façade, when, after starts and stops in traffic, struggles with the steep grades of the hills, and many jolts for shifting gears, the van slowed down, bumped onto what must be a drive or a very secondary road and came to a halt, the motor idling. I got to my feet and glanced out the porthole-like window. We were up in the hills again, late Van Gogh territory, all dry yellows and olive greens; rural life will be the death of me.

Paul stepped out of the van; I heard his feet crunching on gravel. *Pick a door, Francis.* His left, my right. I lifted the can of paint and flattened myself against the right-hand door. A rattle as he moved the latch, a creak as he struggled to open the door; there was something awkward about him that none of his associates had mentioned. I gripped the paint can with both hands and drew it back, ready. When he leaned in, revolver in hand, I threw the paint in his face, a white solvent-laden wave that staggered and blinded him. The gun discharged, the bullet ricocheting off the back of the van. I swung the now empty paint can against his hand, and he dropped the weapon.

I don't think I've ever moved faster. Off the back of the van, round behind Paul, who was clawing at his face and trying to rub the paint from his eyes with his sleeve. I grabbed him by the scruff of the neck, and though he was both taller and heavier, I threw him toward the open door of the van, then grabbed his legs, tipped him in, and slammed the door shut. He had the presence of mind to kick back, trying to force the doors open, but I rammed them into alignment and dropped the latch.

I wiped my paint-covered hands on the grass, then leaned against the van to catch my breath. Right enough, we were out in the back of beyond with nothing but scrub, grass, rocks, and a distant grove of pines that looked no more promising than the rest of the landscape. The high, white sun had dried up the sky, and we were alone with the insect chorus. It would be a long hike back to civilization.

Inside the van, Paul was making a fine row, kicking at the doors, rattling the sides, and enlarging my vocabulary of gutter French. Although the van was sturdy, I had the uneasy feeling that a man described as a top flight mechanic might show more ingenuity than I had. I picked up the revolver, which still had a couple of bullets, and fetched one of the cases. I cocked the weapon, aimed at the big, sturdy lock, and pulled the trigger. Bits of metal and leather sprayed around and left the shattered lock hot to the touch. I flipped open the lid to see neat bundles of francs.

True, French currency was down, but there was enough to make someone a rich man. Well, well. The Chavanels had exercised their agile minds searching for a Swiss account and all the time Paul—or his Madame Renard—had kept the cash on hand. I closed the case and heaved it back up onto the seat. I decided against wasting a bullet on the second case, closed the door, and climbed behind the wheel. I touched the gas pedal, as the motor was beginning to sputter, and the engine returned to a soothing purr.

Behind me, Paul was becoming much more vocal. He'd guessed what the shot was for and wanted to negotiate. He'd belatedly realized that the rear of the van was hot, and he was not in the best of health. He had threats, he had inducements, he had proposals, some of which, sitting as I was in the white heat, began to make sense. This would never do. I closed my eyes for a minute and recalled my night drive with Cybelle. I focused on her struggles with the gears, on the way her left foot had depressed what she consistently referred to as the "goddamn clutch." Could I do worse? I took a breath, released the brake, and began the search for first gear.

Travel is adventure—and so it should be. I got the van rolling, steered us from the wide place where Paul had parked without entering the dreaded reverse, and headed back along the narrow road. I managed second. Beyond that, we could not seem to go any faster, which was fine, considering that we were scraping the bushes and grasses on either side and wallowing from one rut and pothole to the next. Behind me, Paul kept up a steady stream of threats and proposals—no more imperious gestures from him. I would have appreciated a few hints on the higher gears once we reached the road, as well as a little advice on the steep descents and hairpin curves.

But once Paul realized that we were descending toward the sea and town, he shut up. Instead, I began to hear a disagreeable thumping whack against the barrier between us. He'd carried a knife somewhere on his person, and he was using it to make a gap in the plywood directly behind me. *Go faster, Francis, straight to the first little town, the first little tabac, there to pull over and call Hector. First little town. First shop.* The tires squealed around a curve, as I oversteered right into the oncoming lane. Back again, wrestling with the wheel, *but not so far, not so far!* The van got a rear tire on the soft shoulder, and it took all my strength to haul us away from what looked like a bottomless abyss.

We'd begun to accelerate remorselessly, and even the low gear and all my weight on the brake could not slow our descent. The van careened from one side of the road to the other, and to add to the joy, nasty splinters sprayed from a widening hole just to the right of my head. I shrank away from the point of the knife. First little town, I told myself. Paul could stir up a row and alert the citizenry. So be it. First town, first phone, I stopped.

Thwack! A bit lower this time, right at the base of my neck if I was calculating correctly. I was driving a crazy person. A glance in the mirror showed that he'd made a second hole, and from the sound of splintering wood, he was now trying to split the layers of plywood so that he could stab my neck while I was distracted by hairpin bends and the van's tendency to waggle its back end like a rent boy.

No doubt in my place, Paul would have picked up the revolver and fired a warning shot through the barrier, but I didn't dare take a hand off the wheel. No, indeed, so there we were, careening around the bends, slithering between rock and chasm. The slit behind my head widened relentlessly until I felt a sharp prick to the right of my neck, smack in the big trapezius muscle. By sheer reflex, I grabbed at the injury with my left hand, which overbalanced the steering wheel to my right and sent the van roaring toward the edge of a steep drop into rocks and scrub.

A pain in my fingers; hacking away through the gap, Paul had caught my thumb. I jerked my bleeding hand away and grabbed the wheel, but it was too late. This time two tires plowed into the soft shoulder; the van listed crazily and lost the curve. I stood on the brake, but, overbalanced, the van bounced down the slope, scrub clawing at the undercarriage, my stomach clawing at my palate. We'd have dropped right to the bottom, if we hadn't fetched up against a rock outcropping as big as a bus.

I slammed into the steering wheel and my knees cracked the dashboard. It was a moment or two before I realized that we had stopped, perhaps thirty feet below the road, balanced on two wheels at a forty-five-degree angle, with a straight shot down to the next hairpin turn. *Get out of the van, Francis!*

Paul was quiet in the back, but I thought that I could leave a man of his ingenuity to his own devices. I unlatched the driver's-side door and after a struggle against weight and gravity, got it open. I was set to climb out when I remembered the suitcases. Two were more than I could manage, but one seemed a good idea. I stuck Paul's revolver in my waistband, threw the unlocked case from the van, and followed it out. Though the vehicle shivered and dipped, the rock held it fast. I started to clamber back up to the road, but the grade was steeper than I'd realized. Down, then. I let the case go and followed, sliding and stumbling, grasping at branches and roots and rocks all the way to the tarmac below.

Far in the distance, I could see the blue of the sea with a pale ribbon of road snaking down toward it. I hefted the case and set off. I'd maybe walked a mile when the usual insect drone was increased by a metallic whir. I looked back to see a young cyclist descending at reckless speed, crouched over his machine with his dark head down and his rump in the air. The boy leaned into the curves, right, left, then dropped out of sight. He was followed by two, three, a dozen more, all dressed in the same striped shirts Pierre sported. Junior cyclists on a training run.

As the buzz and whir of their derailleurs faded, I heard the sound of a motor. I stepped into the road and waved at a truck loaded with spare bikes. A squeal of brakes and then Pierre's curly head leaned out. "Francis!"

I threw the case in the back, opened the passenger door, and climbed in.

"What are you doing out here?"

"I was chauffeur to a crazy man, but I crashed the van. Long story."

"What's the short version?"

"Serge Brun is dead; we've come into money, and I need to see Hector."

CHAPTER NINETEEN

I wanted nothing more to do with Paul Desmarais, *flics*, or heavy suitcases. I was getting sick of adventures without pleasure, and my small quotient of public-spiritedness was so depleted it was going to take years of self-indulgence to replenish the store. But though I explained this at length to Hector, he still insisted that I come along to help find the van. That my own memory of the journey was spotty to say the least meant little. According to him, everything had shifted into high gear thanks to my adventures in café society, and I was the authorities' fair-haired boy. Did that mean my passport would be returned?

"We're working on that," said Hector.

We went—Hector, Pierre, and me—with two plainclothes

detectives in a big sedan, accompanied by a *flic* on a motorcycle to lend us importance. I had remembered the name of the street where Paul had taken the van, and some functionary was already tracking who owned the building and how it was that my lame abductor had gone there with such confidence. I could not help them on the route into the hills, except to assure them that most of the time I thought we had traveled northwest.

"Why did he stop?" One of the detectives wanted to know. He was very tall and thin with ginger hair and a face raw from the sun, as if his northern pelt had never adapted to the latitude. He sat uncomfortably in back with Pierre and me, on a little jump seat that had his knees keeping company with his chin.

"I believe he intended to kill me."

"Suggesting he no longer needed you to carry the case?" The detective sniffed at this and pursed his lips doubtfully. "Why not at the garage?"

How I love having my demise discussed so casually. "There were other garages and small works around. In the hills, there was nothing but scrub. Who goes up there?"

"You said there was a road."

"A poor excuse for one."

"Yet you were able to drive back without a license." He spoke as if he would like to write me up for that.

"I'd never driven before, but I'd seen people drive. Anyway, I had no choice, as he was trying to smash through the barrier and stab me. Once on the road, it was downhill; all I had to do was steer."

"Not very well," the detective observed. What an ungrateful bunch. They had a witness to Serge Brun's killing, they had evidence of the killer's whereabouts, and they had the murder weapon. They had, in fact, everything but the leather case stuffed with francs currently residing in Hector's closet. I wasn't sure how that was going to come out, though I agreed with Hector and Pierre that those francs would do no good languishing in some evidence room. "Besides," said Hector, "there are still officers on the force nostalgic for the old days."

Right, and Inspector Chardin was one of them. The question was, could I trust these new coppers? Even with Hector's imprimatur, I was apparently unsatisfactory, because I hadn't steered the van direct to their HQ and delivered Paul cleaned of paint and smelling like a rose.

I was preparing to sulk when Pierre interrupted to say that he thought he could estimate where I'd gone off the road. But though the Sud-Est team regularly used that stretch for training, even he did not spot the accident site until we had turned around far up in the hills and started back down again.

I thought I recognized a particularly formidable curve. "We came onto the road near here," I said. I could feel my hands getting sweaty with the memory.

"You came down a fair way," said Pierre.

"It seemed like forever."

Another curve, another hairpin bend. There were no guardrails, and in some places the scrub was so thick it was impossible to see if there had been damage.

"Wait, stop," said Pierre. "Back up."

I got out of the car and went to the edge of the road where the tire marks Pierre had spotted sketched a loose curve in the white dust. "We almost went off here, but not yet. Farther on."

With one of the detectives driving slowly alongside, the rest of us walked down the road, through another turn, then into the sharp drop that I remembered all too well. "Somewhere in here," I said, and Pierre's sharp eyes picked out the tracks, a deeper gouge this time, then a tangle of broken branches. Even so, had we not been looking specifically, we'd almost certainly have missed the van. It was just as I had left it, leaning on two wheels against the big rock, but when we scrambled down the slope, over loose stones and thorny branches, we found the rear doors open.

They were splashed with white paint to confirm my story, and there were white, sticky handprints on the side of the van and on the driver's-side door, as well as two jagged holes hacked out of the plywood divider. But Paul had gotten himself out of the van. He was gone and the second case was, too.

"You said you locked the van doors."

"I secured the latch."

"The doors must have popped open on impact," suggested Pierre.

All these details—and the suspect's absence—were relayed up to the motorcyclist, who roared away down the road.

"We will need a very good description of him," the thin detective said. "As you are the only one to have seen him."

I could see myself once again as a prisoner of the Riviera, mired in doubtful identifications and bound to assist the police. "The cabdriver saw him, too," I said quickly. "I can't remember the name of the company, but there was a palm tree painted on the side of the cab."

The detective made a note of this without ceasing to regard me with deep suspicion. The two coppers examined the van from every angle and traced my path down to the hairpin bend below, but the track plowed by the van and our descent en masse effectively concealed which way Paul had gone.

Hector, Pierre, and I returned to the roadway and waited while the guardians of the law made yet another inspection of the van interior. "I don't think they believe me," I remarked to Hector. "Paul was clearly able to muscle one case to the roadway. And that's after an accident. What did he need me for?" Though it was nice that some ill-gotten gains would go to the deserving, concealing that second case wasn't helping me at all.

"It is a risk," Hector admitted.

"That's not all. If he makes any connection to you or the Chavanels, if he thinks you might have his money, look out."

Hector did not get to answer that, because the detectives were lumbering back up the slope. We drove back into town, where Pierre was excused, and Hector accompanied me to the station to give yet another statement and to look at some old photos of Paul Desmarais.

I turned them over one by one. Same black hair, same black eyes, though the camera had not caught the malevolent expression that had so struck me. His face was a little fuller, remarkable in wartime and indicative of his work in the black market; I couldn't decide about the mouth or nose. "He looks very like that." I said finally. "But did he have a limp? A noticeable awkwardness?"

The detectives shook their heads.

"The man I know as Victor Renard limps."

"You said that he was shot in London."

"In the chest. He was shot in the chest and supposedly died."

"He might have been hit in the leg as well," Hector suggested.

That was possible. In the darkness, I could have missed a leg wound in my concern for the massive bleeding from his chest.

"Yet with all that, he seems to be out and about and killing old associates," said the thin detective.

I found his skepticism worrisome, since I kept winding up compromised by corpses of one sort or another. "Who are killing one another," I added before I caught myself. "I'm thinking, of course, of Madame Renard." *Say no more about that, Francis!*

We went over my visit to the Villa Mimosa again. The detectives weren't getting anywhere. They didn't know about my activities as amateur undertaker, and I hadn't a clue as to what they thought. At last, I was released into Hector's custody with vague promises of progress on my passport, which still resided with Inspector Chardin.

"If he has it, I'll be here forever," I complained to Hector.

"He's one of the people we're looking at. He was an associate of Paul's and a big supporter of the Milice. If he gets his hands on that case, you can be sure it will disappear."

"Everyone wants Paul's money."

"Yes," said Hector. "Even Madame Renard. I wonder where Gustave kept the cash hidden."

"The apartment looked to have been gone through pretty thoroughly. I thought maybe that was Cybèle's work."

"I don't know where Cybèle is," Hector said. "Maybe Paul ripped up the apartment himself, searching."

"Suggesting that 'Madame Renard' had hidden money from him?" That was a possibility and an explanation for entrusting the "last letter" to a jackal like Joubert, but I wasn't convinced. "I don't think so. I heard him moving around upstairs in the night, but not making the sort of clatter the search must have caused. I had the sense that he had tidied the place, swept up the glass and so on, as if the damage offended him."

"Then he must have known where to look."

"I think so, and I'm guessing that he brought the cases with him. And he must have had a key. I climbed in a window, but he is not in such good shape."

"Good enough to kill Serge Brun."

"Yes, and if I were you, I'd get that case out of your house as fast as possible and get me on the boat train tonight before Paul makes the connection."

Hector looked surprised. "Thank you for your concern," he said with the formal politeness the French favor, "but that is impossible.

We have waited years to settle with Paul Desmarais. My hope is that he will come after his money, and I intend to do everything possible to let him know where it is."

I didn't like that at all; I'd really had enough of being the goat that lures the tiger.

"Of course, of course," he said. "It is very bad of us to impose on you again, given that you've taken risks for us already. But," he continued, "it is not totally one sided. Your position is delicate and some of your activities would not withstand closer examination."

I hoped he wasn't threatening me, but I suspected that he was. "My activities involved both Cybèle and Pierre," I said. "Do not expect me to protect them."

Hector looked sad at this, as if disillusioned by the weaknesses in human nature, specifically mine. "I meant only that you still need my help and that my contacts in the Sûreté can protect you somewhat from people like Chardin, who would sacrifice you in a minute to protect old comrades and new rackets."

I apologized for any mistaken insinuation and the two of us exchanged formal expressions of esteem. French is very good for that. It allows one to lay cards on the table without open hostilities.

"My thought," said Hector, "was that we treat Pierre to a fine dinner, perhaps with some of his cycling colleagues. And let it be known."

"Perhaps the restaurant at the Negresco," I said sarcastically.

"The very thing," exclaimed Hector. "That will certainly secure attention. Monsieur, you are a species of genius."

That is how I went from dishwasher to guest at the most expensive hotel in Nice and added entertaining to my previous skills as gravedigger, beachfront artiste, and van driver. Our plans hit a little snag in that the Sud-Est team was pedaling away in the foothills of the Alps and could hardly be released for a slap-up feast with wine at every course. Hector surmounted this problem by inviting the junior team and some of the support personnel, and he saw that the event would be noticed in the local papers.

"Aren't we endangering the boys?" I asked.

"The story will run after the fact," he said and clapped me on the shoulder.

I was still doubtful. Nan, my studio, Arnold, the promising painting with the unsatisfactory background, all seemed increasingly distant. I was no nearer the boat train and home than I had been on the day Inspector Chardin and the handsome officer from Monaco first requested my assistance. I was drinking too much and surly with everyone, until Pierre pulled me aside for a chat.

This was on the train for Nice—where we were going, with my reluctant participation, to finalize the dinner arrangements. "Don't be angry with Hector," Pierre said earnestly.

"I'm not just angry with Hector," I said. "I'm angry with the universe. It's a crazy scheme, and it's not the first one. Virtually, since I arrived in France, people have been asking me to do insane things for someone else's benefit."

"Hector is a fine man," Pierre said.

"A fine man, even remarkable, and the Chavanels are fine women and remarkable, too. Everyone is remarkable, including Cybèle, but they're all obsessed with Paul Desmarais, and the only place I want to see him again is on canvas." Indeed, having said it, I realized that was just the place for him with his dark coat and his sinister eyes. I could see his livid face against a ground between blue and black.

"You would not know this, but he murdered Hector's brother. Claude was a teacher at my school. He taught me, in fact." Pierre looked out at the Mediterranean, silver under clouds and was silent for a moment. "He was a kind, gentle person, totally apolitical. Desmarais tortured him to death as a resistant."

There was no comfort for that and I said nothing.

"That was when we—I mean Cybèle and me, she knew him, too—got involved. Little things. She distributed phony ration coupons so people didn't starve to death, and I ran errands and carried messages, always on the bike. If I was stopped, I said I was out training. I won a local race that year, and some of the Germans made money betting on me. I was their favorite because they knew I trained hard. What do you think of that?"

"I think life is absurd," I said.

He clapped me on the shoulder. "War is shit and life is absurd. So . . . we go and have a good time at the Negresco?"

What could I do but agree? A couple of nights before the arrival of the Tour and of twenty-four-hour days for Pierre, a dozen of us were seated on the terrace of the Negresco, lapped in the velvet Mediterranean night and overlooking the lights of the Promenade des Anglais and the ebony sea. With waiters at hand, our adjoining tables were awash in white linen and monogrammed napkins, with wine bottles in silver ice buckets, fancy hors d'oeuvres, and wonderful rolls, with soup to follow and a choice of entrées and what the management had assured us would be a truly extravagant dessert trolley.

As we demolished course after course, the thin, young racers doing us proud with seconds and thirds, I could not help thinking of the folks down below—Gaston and the Napoleonic chef and the shaky kitchen boy who had made my foray into dishwashing so exciting. The boy would have little to do tonight, as our plates went back bare. After my third glass of excellent Champagne, I told Hector that the party was a brilliant idea and after my fifth, I really believed it.

"You are a comrade for all occasions," Hector said. Possibly he meant it, too, because although he hadn't lost his alert expression, he had joined me in his admiration of the fine wine. We got back to town late and full of merriment, and I must say that Paul Desmarais treated me to the finest dinner I've ever had

"Now we wait," said Hector the next morning. He'd insisted that I stay at his house, where he presented me with a MAS 1873 revolver, an officer's pistol from the trenches of World War I—wouldn't Nan be impressed by that. He regaled me with its long history and widespread use, ending with recent service to the police and the Resistance, and showed me how to use it.

"Double action," he said. "You can't fire it by mistake."

I found this detail comforting, and he assured me it was easy in the hand, which I hoped I wouldn't need to discover. Then he insisted on coffee at the local *tabac*, where we fielded questions about the dinner party, already a subject of speculation.

"Eh, Hector. You've dug up the *Boche* gold!" called one old gaffer.

"In a manner of speaking." Hector winked. He was happy to confirm all the details of our gala, while skillfully deflecting any questions about how such a party had been funded. This tactic ensured that everything from the wine list to the tips for the waiters would be a subject of discussion as soon as we were out the door. "Paul will hear of it," Hector said with satisfaction. "Before the day is out, I would guess."

"You think he is still in the area?"

"Why not? He wants that case—we're not even sure what's in the other one. Might be personal effects for all we know."

"No, too heavy. If I were him, I'd cut my losses and leave France."

"But you're not him. I think Joubert betrayed him. Therefore, he will want to kill Joubert. And Brun and his friends killed Madame Renard. Therefore, he wanted to eliminate them. That is how his mind works."

"Suggesting that I am next on the list."

"We have joined a select group," Hector admitted. "But do not worry. This time we will get him. He escaped us at the end of the war, but now there are no Yanks with trucks for him to hide among. I am not the only one looking for him, either." He patted my shoulder again. "The MAS is a fine weapon. Keep it with you."

CHAPTER TWENTY

"I am worried about Pierre," I told Hector. "He could hardly be more visible." We were maintaining our high profile for a second day, eating lunch at a good hotel restaurant on the main boulevard. We sat out on the terrace, ordered up three courses, and finished with liqueurs. Hector indulged in a cigar, and we looked the picture of prosperity. Untroubled prosperity, I might add. Despite Hector's confidence in his plan, we had not heard from Paul Desmarais. No mysterious shadows had appeared beneath Hector's windows, and when I'd lingered in the café until late, the MAS tucked into my waistband, no one had accosted me on the way back to Hector's small house. Here we were lazing under the plane trees, while Pierre, having joined his Sud-Est team, was up in the hinterlands with the cyclists racing toward us from the Alpes-Maritimes .

"There is no reason to think Pierre is a target. And he is surrounded by the team and the other mechanics." Hector watched the fragrant blue smoke of his cigar ascend against the pale underbellies of the leaves. "I could learn to enjoy this." He smiled sadly. "When I was with the Sûreté, I considered that evidence was sacred. The war has left us all more flexible."

"And you are no longer a policeman."

"True, still . . ." He paused, and I wondered if he had developed some doubts about his plan.

"Was there any alternative?"

"Hardly. I don't think you could fund dinners at the Negresco."

"The only other time I was there, I was washing dishes."

"Really? I'm sure there's a story."

"One I'm not going to tell just yet." I took another sip of my crème de cassis and saw, to my regret, that the glass was empty. I would have liked another, but Hector said that we had to start walking. The racers would not turn onto the coastal road until the next town, and though he knew the best spot to see the cyclists, we had to be in good time to get a place.

Hector paid the bill, tipping the waiter enough extra to be notable, and we set off along the handsome palm-lined boulevard. I thought it unfortunate that the race had not chosen such a splendid street, but Hector pointed out that its sudden narrowing in the twists and turns by the casino would be too dangerous for a mass of cyclists. Instead, the racers would drop down out of the hills, turn onto the main street of Fréjus, and head along the coast. His chosen viewing spot was right near the bottom of the hill leading to the shore. There, we could see the descent, the turn onto the main street, and even catch a glimpse of a sprint point in town.

Other aficionados had the same idea, and we had to search for a spot. We finally settled on a low wall on the land side of the road where one frail tree provided a tiny patch of broken shade. Then we waited. Once in a while the sea breeze stirred the hot, still air; cicadas called monotonously from a patch of scrub. Out on the Mediterranean, sailboats drifted like butterflies, and the water turned from turquoise to deep blue in the distance.

An enterprising gent brought his cart of Italian ices up from the beach and set up shop just across the street from us. As I watched him dealing out the multicolored scoops, I decided that the heat would be unendurable without an ice. Hector declined, but I crossed the road and joined the line moving slowly toward the vendor's brightly painted handcart.

Customers wanted *fraise*, they wanted chocolate, they couldn't decide between *limon* and cassis. They needed a cone for themselves and another twenty relatives. A gendarme passed in a police car, the first indication that the race was approaching. Customers now wanted their cones faster, and there was a bit of shoving in line. I was pushed into the man behind me, who caught my shoulder and kept me from falling just as we heard the roar of the motorcycle escorts. Far up the hill, the first of the racers, still just bright flecks of color at this distance, shot down the slope.

"*Pardonnez-moi, monsieur. Merci.*"

The man behind me patted my shoulder. "*C'est toujours comme ça,*" he said and stepped to the side to give me a little more room in the queue. That's when I saw Paul. He was standing farther back on the sidewalk with his right hand in his jacket pocket, and he'd seen me. Yes, he had, and though I had that excellent weapon, the MAS 1873 revolver, my immediate impulse was to leave the area. I heard the whir of derailleurs as the breakaway riders slowed a fraction for the turn then charged onto the street to cheers and shouts.

The peloton was in pursuit and closing fast, but I dashed across the street, bouncing into fans on the other side, who angrily shoved me back through the crowd. Hector jumped down from his perch on the wall. "What in hell are you doing? You could have hit a racer."

"I saw Paul; I'm sure he's armed."

The words were barely out of my mouth before we heard a crash and shouts and the nasty rattle, whir, and thump of bodies and machines in collision. I followed Hector as he shoved his way to the street. A dozen or so racers had gone down. A couple were already struggling to their feet and trying to right their machines. Others lay on the pavement or sat holding bleeding heads or cradling injured arms. Paul lay among them, not moving. He had one hand outstretched and his legs were entangled with the wheel and frame of a damaged machine. There was blood on his face, and he was lying at a bad angle.

I moved to examine him, but Hector clutched my shoulder, more riders coming. Their brakes squealed as they wove back and forth to avoid the fallen cyclists, and some unlucky competitors joined the injured in the street. The rest bent over their machines and accelerated away. Mobile riders began moving their damaged bikes to the side, or, if the machines were operational, climbed on again, their legs and arms scraped and bleeding, while fans got behind and pushed to give them a start.

With all this confusion and the support vans approaching, it was a minute or two before Hector could step into the street and shout for a gendarme and an ambulance. Then the crowd noticed the fallen man, dressed in a jacket and trousers instead of the bright uniforms of the Tour. Hector shouted everyone back, but I moved forward. Life had gone into reverse, and I was back at the portico of the gambling club with a man in a blue overcoat bleeding in the road.

"He is alive," I said. "I need something for the blood. Towels, handkerchiefs."

"The race doctor will be here soon," Hector said, and though the crowd wanted to move Paul, we resisted. Support vans with honking horns were backed up along the road. Calls for the doctor were passed up the line of vehicles, and various mechanics and team managers jumped out of their cars and trucks to see what had happened and where their racers were. Some of the riders were shouting for spare wheels or spare bikes, and frantic mechanics were running with new equipment. The gendarmes' car couldn't get by, and Hector pushed through the crowd to find them.

I stayed with Paul, trying to stanch the blood that poured from his head wound with my pocket handkerchief and shouting for the doctor. At this moment, Pierre appeared, carrying two spare wheels and wearing a garland of new inner tubes. "Francis! What's happened?"

At that moment, I felt Paul move; he lifted his hand, still in his jacket pocket, and there was a short, sharp sound. Pierre staggered and cried out in pain; someone in the crowd screamed a warning. Paul had a dark, snub-nosed pistol out of his pocket now, and I grabbed for his wrist and held on while he struggled to get off another shot, the pistol waving up and down. The crowd scattered with shouts and cries, pushing and shoving and stumbling against the wall and over the curbing, before one of the mechanics, wheeling in a fresh bike, saw what was happening and kicked him hard in the side.

Paul's body jumped against me, before I felt him go limp. The pistol dropped to the tarmac, and I shoved it beyond his reach. Paul Desmarais was never again to see the light, but at the moment all my concern was for Pierre, who sat on the pavement, his eyes wide with pain and surprise, blood streaming over the shreds of the inner tubes around his neck. I pulled off my jacket and ripped off my shirt. One of the spectators pulled the bits of rubber away from the wound, and I pressed the shirt against what seemed a flood of red. Had Paul's wild shot hit the carotid artery? Was this to be his revenge on the most innocent of us all? With trailing cyclists still maneuvering around us, I pressed frantically on the wound, but now Pierre winced. "I think it broke my collarbone," he said with a gasp. "Cyclist's injury and I wasn't even on the bike."

"Stay still, stay still. We need to get the bleeding stopped," I said, but I was heartened that he was making even feeble jokes. Perhaps the thick rubber tubes had dampened the force of the bullet, but even so, there was a lot of blood. When Hector saw it, he went quite white. "I'm so sorry," he said to Pierre. "So very sorry." Then he jumped up to find the race doctor, who finally arrived, wheezing and puffing from a long run down the line of backed-up support vehicles. He sloshed water on the wound, revealing a red furrow running from the collarbone up along the neck muscles, a large, nasty wound but fortunately not deep.

"He thinks the bone may be broken," I said.

The doctor, elderly and stout with long white hair and little gold-rimmed glasses, poked and probed before pronouncing his assent. He took bandages and a sling from his medical bag and soon had Pierre's right arm immobilized and a thick white bandage affixed to his neck. By this time, the gendarmes and ambulance men had arrived. One of the medical men checked for Paul's pulse then shook his head. A few minutes later, the body was loaded onto a stretcher. When a gendarme recovered the pistol and began to collect statements from the crowd, I took the opportunity to ask if I could accompany Pierre in the team car. "I will see that he gets home from the railroad station."

Pierre looked set to protest that he was fine, just shaken up, that he wanted to accompany the team. Then he saw the gendarmes with their notebooks and their eager curiosity and said, "That would be good. I don't need an ambulance but I feel quite sick."

I took one arm and the old doctor took the other. "Later, later," he said to the gendarme, and we led Pierre back up the road to the Sud-Est truck and helped him in. The cop might have protested, but Hector drew him aside. They were still talking earnestly when we drove past the heap of damaged bikes and the bloodstained pavement.

My passport, my own passport, was in my pocket along with my tickets and a wire from Arnold promising to meet my train and informing me that Monsieur Joubert, aka László Bencze, had been arrested on a charge of threatening and that Nan was enthusiastic about a civil prosecution. You can see why I am reluctant to leave her alone for any length of time, but Hector and Pierre agreed that this was very satisfactory news.

We had all gone north together to Caen so that Pierre could see the start of the final day. He had been bitterly disappointed to miss the coastal stages, having been judged too weak to ride in the uncomfortable Sud-Est support van. This trip was the consolation prize. On the way, Hector filled us in with all the new information he possessed. Of course, the police—or at least some of them— were pleased. Paul and Serge Brun were not only gone, but several outstanding cases had been cleared. There seemed little doubt that Brun was responsible for the body at the Villa Mimosa and no doubt at all that Paul had shot him.

Several other well-known thugs had disappeared without a trace and, perhaps wisely, the authorities had decided to treat this as a bonus, not a puzzle. I was relieved at that and Pierre was, too. I was only sorry that Cybèle did not know. "Cybèle will not be back,"

Hector told us. "Not for a while, I don't think. She's all right," he said, seeing my expression. "She wanted a new life, a new start. Now she has it."

"She seized Paul's account, then?"

"I believe so, but I will know more when the Chavanel ladies return."

I was sorry to have missed them. "But will they be safe? There's still Madame Lambert."

"I doubt she will return with warrants for her arrest in France."

Pierre seemed to think this was right and turned our conversation to the race. Though the experts gave the nod to the Italian, Brambilla, who'd taken the lead with the nineteenth stage time trial, Pierre still cherished hopes of a French victory, especially with the start at Caen. "That will be worth a minute or two to any Frenchman," he said confidently, but when the train pulled into the shattered and rubble-strewn center, he and Hector were stunned. The south had seen nothing like the Allied bombing of Caen. I came from a different place, and though horrified, I recognized familiar territory, right down to the smell of pulverized brick and stone, and the omnipresent scaffolding, excavations, and cranes.

"The whole city is like the dockyards," I told them. "It is like the dockyards during the Blitz."

Against the pale, bleached rubble, the water-filled bomb craters, and blackened timbers, the colors of the racing strips seemed almost unnaturally brilliant. Spectators were arranged in little groups all along the roads. They cheered and shouted for Brambilla and Robic, Ronconi, Vietto, and Fachleitner, for Italia and France and Pierre's Sud-Est squad—and for the hopes of an ordinary life where cyclists again whirred down intact streets. A rush of pleasure accompanied the riders, many of whom waved as they passed, yet the atmosphere was very different from the festive crowd in Fréjus.

There was something solemn underneath, a mix of determination and exhaustion that made me feel at home, too.

Then in a moment, the bright peloton was gone, along with the motorcycles, support cars, and trucks. Pierre looked so white and tired that we took him directly to the station. I had a connection for Rouen and Dieppe, and they hoped to get to Paris in time for the final sprint on the Champs-Elysées. I hugged them both, and we promised to write, though I think all of us doubted that would happen.

"I will keep you informed," said Hector.

As I made my way to my compartment, I wondered about that as well. There were, from first to last, a number of things I hadn't been told and too many loose ends remained for me to feel entirely happy. How could I be with three Madame Renards, a Monsieur Renard who never was, five corpses, one not yet identified, and a man literally returned from the dead? What didn't I know? Let me tote it up: Why had Paul entrusted his documents to a rascal like Joubert, or alternately, how had Joubert gotten the notebook and letter away from him? And what of Serge Brun of the protection racket and dodgy clubs? Another man with a history to make you dizzy.

All I could be sure of was that, after Paul Desmarais was shot in London, Joubert secured the notebook and letter, hoping to track their delivery to "Madame Renard" by yours truly. Serge Brun, who, like Joubert, had a profitable war and mysterious connections in café society, got wind of the scheme and murdered poor Madame Renard the First, aka Gustave Gravois, aka that great drag singer Mademoiselle Veronique, and substituted Cybèle, who got the package and almost wound up herself in the fish locker. A timely intervention by my first alter ego, Marcel Lepage, stopped that!

Paul, meanwhile, was back on his feet and out for revenge—and for the suitcases his old lover Mademoiselle Veronique had stashed for him. He'd have gotten clean away if my second alter ego, Eugène, hadn't fancied singing lessons, which just goes to show that chance rules us all, even homicidal schemers like Paul Desmarais. Yes, indeed. And I haven't even touched on who tried to stab me or whether the Chavanels really did break Paul's bank code.

I doubted that I'd ever know more, but I was going home, back to Nan, whom I love and who would be entertained for weeks with these problems, and back to Arnold, who is good for me and who would give me sage advice, and back to painting, which I need like food and sex and drink, with new ideas and a couple of strange new images.

The train drew away from the platform, and I resolved to put doubts and questions behind me. My friends had survived; my enemies were vanquished. I was done with Marcel Lepage, furniture restorations, and genealogy, as well as with the unlamented Eugène Laroche, he of the smart repartee and the bizarre desire to sing lieder. I was well rid of them, and I decided to celebrate with a fine meal, which, thanks to a little last-minute largesse from Hector, I could well afford.

Into the restaurant car with its white tablecloths and uniformed waiters, one of whom indicated a seat near the entrance. The other tables held prosperous-looking businessmen and stylish couples and, far to the back, a single woman with a large black picture hat shadowing her face. I nodded a greeting to the assembled and focused on the menu: leek and potato soup—one of my favorites. *Coq au vin* with green beans and *pommes frites*. Also very nice. A *pêche melba* for dessert. There were things about France that I certainly would miss. The wines, too, of course. I ordered a bottle of white Burgundy, a pale-gold-and-green-tinged liquid that helped speed me along the French countryside. Some of the fields were planted; some were still stripped of trees and shattered like the killing fields of the First World War. I made a mental note to tell Nan.

I lingered at the table, any nagging discontent soothed with the fine vintage, and it was to prolong this pleasure that I ordered coffee and a liqueur. By the time I was finished, we were outside Rouen and headed north to Dieppe and the ferry. I started back to my compartment, walking a trifle unsteadily across the swaying connections between the cars. My seat was in the fourth car from the restaurant, and I had just reached the door of the second, when I felt something hard in the small of my back.

"Stop right there, Monsieur."

Quite irrationally, I thought of my undertaking duties and jumped in alarm. I say irrationally, because the voice, though low and rather harsh, was definitely feminine. When I turned my head, I saw the black picture hat with a drooping ostrich feather. Underneath was a thin face with red lipstick and malevolent dark eyes. Yvette Lambert suddenly looked a great deal like her brother.

"On your way to the coast ahead of the gendarmes?" I asked to give myself a little time. "Off perhaps to England and points west?"

"Go to the door."

I started toward the next compartment and felt the gun in my kidney. "The exit door," she said.

I didn't like this at all.

"Put down the window and hurry up."

I lowered the window that occupied the upper half of the door. We were zipping through open fields bordered by thick hedgerows. The track was lined with crushed rock and bordered by shrubs and long grass.

"Jump," she said.

I was so surprised that I forgot the gun and turned around to look at her. "Whatever for?"

"My brother," she said. "This is for my brother."

Just when I'd almost regained the illusion of normal life, I discover that, besides their other excesses, my French acquaintances believe in blood vengeance. I attempted righteous indignation. "As a matter of fact, I saved your brother's life in London. He'd have bled to death if I hadn't known first aid."

"Your friends shot him."

"Arnold had nothing to do with it."

"Arnold, who is this Arnold? I'm talking about Hector and the bicycle boy. Didn't you know? Oh, I see you didn't. They'd plotted for years."

I realized with a shock that was plausible, very plausible—*but don't admit that now, Francis.* "I'd have thought your late pal, Serge Brun, a better bet." Sooner or later someone would pass in the corridor, perhaps even one of the officious conductors. I only had to spin out the time. "And he had other enemies. Your husband's grandfather, for one."

"Yes, and he bankrolled the attack. He certainly did, though he plays with model houses and innuendo and walks with his nose in the air as if he'd never handled shit. I know he paid Hector and the bicycle boy to go to London. How else would they have gotten the money? A man on a small pension and a bike repairman with a mortgaged shop? No, Monsieur, and because they are beyond reach, you must jump. Or I shoot. Now open the door."

I hesitated. Would she shoot? I decided she would. Could I survive the jump? Probably not. But I probably wouldn't survive a shot at this range, either. The train doors opened from the outside; I reached out the window and turned the handle. The wind caught the door, banging it open flat against the side of the train. I descended one step, grabbed the vertical handrail next to the opening and swung away from the doorway.

Was this a good idea? I could see the ground flowing white,

gray, and brown beneath my feet; the grass by the track was a green ribbon waving at oblivion.

"Jump!" she said. "Jump!" She stepped into the doorway and raised the gun.

I got a death grip on the handrail and swung toward her with both feet in the air. Perhaps we passed over some points or started into a turn, for I was already in motion when the carriage suddenly swayed. The gun discharged, but Yvette, stylishly dressed in high heels, lost her balance. She grabbed for the rail, for me, for the door, but with another rumble, the train shook her off like a horse with a fly. She was airborne and flowing backward with the ground, the grass. I heard a thump and then the train bent away on its tracks, and she disappeared.

I was left hanging from the handrail, the sleepers and gravel inches from my feet. My arms felt like jelly, but to fall now would be ridiculous. Wheezing and gasping, I hauled myself up level with the bottom step and got first one, then the other foot on the metal. I took a breath—never very deep with my asthmatic lungs—and risked taking one hand off the rail. My body gave a nasty dip toward the ground before I grabbed the doorframe. I pulled myself inside and stood in the open doorway, gasping and sweating. Then I closed the door and the window and staggered, rubber legged, to my compartment.

Fortunately, it was momentarily empty. I collapsed on the seat and gasped until my lungs calmed down. Then I straightened my tie, brushed off my jacket and trousers, wiped my face and hands. By the time the other passengers drifted in, I was leaning against the glass in a good imitation of postprandial drowsiness—*avoid eye contact, Francis*—and trying to make sense of the situation.

The last of Paul Desmarais's associates was gone. He'd been the dying lion with his suitcases of cash and his Swiss account; his sister and Brun and Joubert were the jackals who'd come to feed on the carcass. What were they owed? Not much from me.

And Hector and Pierre? Could Yvette have been right, that Old Lambert had put aside his distaste for mechanics and paid the two of them? Was his violent reaction to Pierre just a ruse? Maybe. And could Hector have been the figure glimpsed from the portico of the gambling club? He was, as Shakespeare says, a man for all weathers, able to organize an ambush, an identity, or a dye job with equal aplomb. He had his reasons, and he admitted himself that his morals had become more flexible with the war. I could see everything but that a man of his capabilities would have failed to kill Paul outright. In Hector's favor, I sincerely doubted that.

Then what about Pierre? A distasteful idea, but though I was reluctant to recast him as an assassin, I remembered his saying, "They are after me, too," at Cannes. Fit and strong, he could have been the figure racing across the road to the saloon car—or the driver waiting inside. He could have been, and that raised questions about our fortuitous meeting on the road below the Villa Mimosa.

I was on the verge of total skepticism when I remembered how embarrassed Pierre had been when I showed up at his bike shop. Had there been some grand design, he would have been eager to see me, and he would have had a very good reason to lie to the police and to keep me from the clutches of the corrupt Inspector Chardin. No, I could not think quite so badly of Pierre. Which didn't mean that he and Hector were innocent; rather that, like the rest of us, they mostly worked by improvisation. The London shooting? There were three or four candidates and for my friends, I gave a Scots verdict: not proven.

Just the same, I'd probably have worried the issue longer if I hadn't been distracted by anxiety. Had some drowsy businessman seen Yvette Lambert's precipitous departure from the Dieppe express? Was he even now searching out the conductor? Or had some old lady glanced from her knitting to see a black hat with an ostrich feather and something—could it be a woman—beside the tracks? Was she alerting her companions and asking if they should pull the alarm?

Excitement for sure, and for yours truly, too. I kept one eye on the corridor, expecting alarms and an unscheduled stop, expecting the conductor, expecting questions, expecting, somewhat irrationally, the police, until, as we approached Dieppe, I began to have real hopes of the crossing and of leaving France behind.

Of course, a good citizen would pull the emergency cord or summon the conductor for a quiet word. A good citizen would miss his connection to the boat train and home. As I watched the rolling land and caught the first faint whiffs of sea air, I thought how fortunate I was to be a bad citizen. I'd been a prisoner of the Riviera and escaped. I decided not to judge my friends, who'd been in a difficult place in a difficult time, and I owed my enemies nothing, not even another clandestine burial. This time I was not going to assist the police with their inquiries; this time I was going home.

THE FRANCIS BACON MYSTERIES

FROM MYSTERIOUSPRESS.COM
AND OPEN ROAD MEDIA

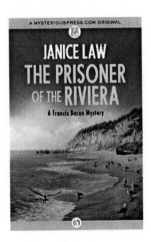

Available wherever ebooks are sold

MYSTERIOUSPRESS.COM

Otto Penzler, owner of the Mysterious Bookshop in Manhattan, founded the Mysterious Press in 1975. Penzler quickly became known for his outstanding selection of mystery, crime, and suspense books, both from his imprint and in his store. The imprint was devoted to printing the best books in these genres, using fine paper and top dust-jacket artists, as well as offering many limited, signed editions.

Now the Mysterious Press has gone digital, publishing ebooks through **MysteriousPress.com**.

MysteriousPress.com offers readers essential noir and suspense fiction, hard-boiled crime novels, and the latest thrillers from both debut authors and mystery masters. Discover classics and new voices, all from one legendary source.

FIND OUT MORE AT

WWW.MYSTERIOUSPRESS.COM

FOLLOW US:

@emysteries and Facebook.com/MysteriousPressCom

MysteriousPress.com is one of a select group of publishing partners of Open Road Integrated Media, Inc.

OPEN ROAD
INTEGRATED MEDIA

Open Road Integrated Media is a digital publisher and multimedia content company. Open Road creates connections between authors and their audiences by marketing its ebooks through a new proprietary online platform, which uses premium video content and social media.

Videos, Archival Documents, and New Releases

Sign up for the Open Road Media newsletter and get news delivered straight to your inbox.

Sign up now at
www.openroadmedia.com/newsletters

CPSIA information can be obtained at www.ICGtesting.com
Printed in the USA
BVOW02s0737231113

337017BV00002B/3/P